BASKETBALL JONES

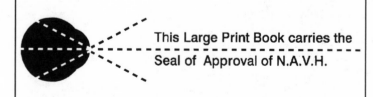

This Large Print Book carries the
Seal of Approval of N.A.V.H.

BASKETBALL JONES

E. LYNN HARRIS

THORNDIKE PRESS
A part of Gale, Cengage Learning

x

GALE
CENGAGE Learning™

Detroit • New York • San Francisco • New Haven, Conn • Waterville, Maine • London

GALE
CENGAGE Learning™

Thorndike Press® Large Print African-American.

The text of this Large Print edition is unabridged.

Other aspects of the book may vary from the original edition.

Set in 16 pt. Plantin.

Printed on permanent paper.

LIBRARY OF CONGRESS CATALOGING-IN-PUBLICATION DATA

Harris, E. Lynn.
  Basketball Jones / by E. Lynn Harris.
    p. cm. — (Thorndike Press large print African-American)
  ISBN-13: 978-1-4104-1266-9 (alk. paper)
  ISBN-10: 1-4104-1266-0 (alk. paper)
    1. African American gays — Fiction. 2. African American bisexuals — Fiction. 3. Basketball players — Fiction. 4. Basketball stories. 5. Large type books. I. Title.
  PS3558.A64438B37 2009b
  813'.54—dc22

                                                    2008043146

Published in 2009 by arrangement with Doubleday, part of the Doubleday Publishing Group, a division of Random House, Inc.

Printed in the United States of America
1 2 3 4 5 6 7 12 11 10 09 08

Dedicated to
Friends for life

Anthony Q. Bell
Carlton A. Brown
Kenneth Hatten
Christopher Martin

Thanks for always being there
even when you're not

ACKNOWLEDGMENTS

Like the words from one of my favorite hymns, I'm truly blessed and duly grateful to publish another novel.

I'm blessed to have a God who provides my every need and stories I can share.

I'm grateful for my family (all of them), especially my mother, Etta W. Harris, my aunt Jessie Phillips, my son, Brandon, and godson, Sean. Also my nieces Bria, Whitney, and Jasmine, and my nephew Bryson for helping me to keep a young spirit.

I'm blessed with wonderful friends. Among them, Vanessa Gilmore, Sean James, Anthony Bell, Carlton Brown, Lencola Sullivan, Cindy and Steven Barnes, Robin Walters, Pamela Fraizer, Derrick and Sonya Gragg, Pam and Donnie Simpson, Sybil Wilkes, Yolanda Sparks, Ken Hatten, Reggie Van Lee, Tony and Brenda Van Putten, Blanche Richardson, Christopher Martin, Proteus Spann, Debra Martin-Chase, Kim and Will Roby, Victoria Christopher Murray, Troy Danato, Kevin Edwards, Tracy and David Huntley, Roy Johnson, Janet Hill, R. M. Johnson, and Dyanna Williams.

I'm grateful for my family at the University of Arkansas-Fayetteville. Especially Jean Nail, David and Jane Gearheart, and the U. of A. Spirit Squads.

I'm blessed with the best publisher and people in the business. They include: Stephen Rubin, Stacy Creamer, Alison Rich, Andrea Dunlop, Meredith McGinnis, Michael Palgon, Bill Thomas, Pauline James, Gerry Triano, Dorothy Boyajy, John Fontana, Christian Nwachukwu Jr., Laura Swerdloff, and Travers Johnson. Special mention to my former editor Janet Hill, who started with me on this novel and is truly missed.

I'm grateful for my necessary support team. Agents, John Hawkins and Moses Cardona. Lawyer, Amy Goldson. Accountants, Bob Braunschweig, Barbara Sussman, and Richard Goldenberg. Outside editors, Don Weise and Chandra Sparks Taylor, who help me mold the book into shape. My assistants, Celia Anderson and Addis (AJ) Huyler, who try their best to keep my life in order. A special thanks to Trina and Jeff Winn, who are like members of my family.

Finally I'm thankful for bookstores, booksellers, book clubs, my students, radio stations, and all the readers who have supported me with love and prayers my entire career. Thank you from the bottom of my grateful and blessed heart.

PROLOGUE

Can you keep a secret? Well, I, Aldridge James Richardson (AJ on the short), can. I've been doing it for so long it's become second nature. I'm not a secretive person either. That came in time. Seven years to be exact. That's how long I've been with Dray Jones. It's for him — for us, really — that I keep all the secrets that allow us to stay a couple. I don't mean ordinary secrets like "Where were you last night?" "Working late," you say, when in reality you're out with the bois. No, I'm talking career-destroying secrets that can make or break a guy and destroy a family. Stuff that, if word got out, your life is basically over — or in my case "our" life would be over, because Dray and I are in this together. Not that we're in any real danger of having our secrets exposed. We're extremely careful to make certain that never happens. Dray knows I love him with all my heart and that I'll keep quiet as long as he needs me to.

But this hasn't been a cakewalk for me. Truth be told, there are times I think I'll burst from holding so much inside. Watching his back and mine is full-time work — a job made no easier by having to keep everything to myself. If there were just one person I could confide in, then some of the weight would be taken off my shoulders. Only I don't dare breathe a word of our business to anyone, not even my best friend or my mother. Instead I spend my life dancing around the truth with the grace of a prima ballerina. The things we do in the name of love!

I don't want to mislead you: I wouldn't have it any other way. I'll do whatever it takes — and have *done* whatever it takes — to be with my first and only true love. That probably sounds romantic and sentimental, like the kind of melodrama that plays out only in tearjerkers. But I really do think of us that way. At the same time, I hope that with all the secrets and the truths not getting told I'm not kidding myself. I sometimes wonder if I've created this romantic image of our relationship to endure the demands our life together requires. It's been so long since we first met that I can't say for sure.

Dray, or Drayton, as his parents named him, wasn't always a big basketball star hiding out from his adoring fans, and I wasn't the boyfriend in the background who pretended to be the star's buddy for their benefit. I fell in love with him in college, back when he didn't have a pot to piss in or a window to throw it out. That's real talk, people. I'd never before been involved with a DLB — otherwise known as a "down low brother" — but knew enough to guess that this probably spelled trouble. At first I wasn't so willing to compromise myself. I've known I was gay my whole life and didn't go out of my way to hide it. That meant I wasn't prepared to help someone else hide his sexuality. But Dray didn't see it like that. He wasn't gay, he assured me. He pointed out the obviously gay men on campus, and would say, "See? That's gay. I'm not like that." Never mind that I was gay and I wasn't like that either. When it came to discussing who or what Dray was, you didn't ask and he didn't tell. In time it made less of a difference to me what he called himself or what people might make of our relationship if they ever found out about it.

We met when I was a senior at Clemson University. I was just a year away from getting my degree in architectural design and Dray was a five-star freshman point guard from Vicksburg, Mississippi, struggling with college algebra. I was hired by the athletic department to tutor him. For a semester our relationship was strictly business. Three nights a week I taught Dray math like he was learning it for the first time. He was an attentive student, but he was more interested in learning what he needed to know about managing his money once he went professional — and there was no doubt in his mind that he would — after a year of college basketball.

Let me say right here that Dray was drop-dead gorgeous. I don't mean run-of-the-mill handsome, but a real knockout for a man. With graham-cracker skin, bow lips, and thick lashes that curled at the ends, he had me ready to lie down at his feet from the word go. The only thing that stood in the way — apart from his being straight and off-limits — was that Dray thought he was slick. He believed there was no one he could not charm or any situation he could not talk himself out of, and at first that ego turned me off. I discovered just how smooth he thought he was when he used a little innocent flirting to try to persuade me to sign in and take a test for him. You know I fought like hell not to fall for his come-on. Although he had no way of knowing it, he had me in his grip so badly that I'd have done backflips over a bed of rocks if he'd asked. But I came to my senses and told him flat-out that there was no way I was going to be part of his scheme, adding that he'd better not try talking some silly girl into taking the test for him, because if he did I'd turn them both in. I took the honor code seriously.

It took my threat to cut through that slick veneer. For the first time, Dray understood that I wasn't just another hustle but someone who took pride in his work. I could see that he was surprised and flattered that his passing the course actually mattered to me. Well, he jumped into his studies with the determination of a star athlete. He not only blocked out time on weekends to devote to algebra, he took the additional step of buying flash cards to improve his retention. He couldn't wait to impress me with the latest lesson he'd learned. Naturally I had no trouble lavishing him with attention, which he ate up as if he'd never been praised for his intellect. This new spirit touched me, and I found it harder than ever not to fall for him. I had a history of falling for straight guys, especially athletes, so I reminded myself that these feelings led nowhere but heartache. Besides, with final exams nearing, it was only a matter of days before my job with him was over and we'd part for good. In the meantime I immersed myself in my own studies to put him out of my head.

As it happened, things weren't that simple. Once classes let out for Christmas break, I flew home to North Carolina to visit my family — and to forget about Dray. I managed to do that for the most part, spending my days shopping with my little sister and enjoying my mother's incredible home cooking. But I couldn't leave him behind entirely. A television character in a syndicated sitcom that ran nightly looked a lot like Dray, and I was reminded of him every time the actor appeared. His character's signature line was "Do yo thang, playa," and each time this was said, he looked into the camera as if speaking directly to me. I grabbed a book and spent the rest of the week avoiding TV during that particular half hour.

My first night back in my studio apartment, there was a knock at the door. The clock said it was half past ten, so I thought it had to be the crabby engineering student next door who sometimes complained when my music was a bit loud. There wasn't any music playing, however, so I couldn't imagine what his problem was this time. I opened the door and, if it had been my own father, I wouldn't have been more surprised. There stood Dray, holding out a slip of paper in one hand and a paper bag in the other. He wore a very sexy gap-toothed grin that practically made me melt right there in the doorway.

Startled to see him so unexpectedly and thrilled to find him at my apartment, I asked with a laugh of disbelief what he was doing there.

He handed me the slip and with a playful slap on my shoulder said, "Take a look, boi." It was his grade card, with a big letter B circled in blue ink.

"Dray, you passed!"

"I didn't just pass, I got a B, dude!" He laughed. "Can you believe it? I've never gotten anything higher than a C in my life, least of all in math. Come on, this calls for a celebration."

"Why do we need to celebrate? You're the one who worked his ass off."

"Because I couldn't have done it without you, dude. But it's not just the grade I'm so excited about. Seriously, if I hadn't passed, I might not be playin' this semester. That would hurt the team and my chances to be a first-round pick for the NBA." As if suddenly remembering he was holding a bag, he said, "Hey, I brought you something." He reached in and pulled out a six-pack of Coronas. "Aren't you going to ask me in?"

I wondered what I might be getting myself into by inviting him in. Was this visit all about college algebra, or had Dray been doing some personal math in his head while I was away? Straight guys don't just show up at a gay man's place late at night with a six-pack of beer. You didn't have to be a genius to know two and two makes four. But that wasn't my only concern. Being conscientious of boundaries, I also asked myself if fraternizing with a student broke any rules set up by the athletic program. Dray wasn't in my charge any longer, so technically we were cool. I thought, "What the fuck," and let him in.

Fast-forward a couple of hours. After Dray's third beer and my second, we stretched out on the Pottery Barn jute rug and fell asleep. Actually, he dropped off first, and I, lulled by the alcohol and the sound of Dray snoring, soon followed. About a half hour later, I opened my eyes and found myself staring into his childlike face. His mouth hung wide open with a tiny trickle of saliva drooling down his chin. Here at last was the slick ballplayer with his guard down. A handsome man-child. But even in that condition — or perhaps because of it — he looked so damned adorable.

I moved in nearer and lay down right beside him, just a breath's distance from his face. I couldn't resist the opportunity to admire his beauty more closely than I'd ever been allowed to see it. I lay there alone in my own private world, watching Dray's peaceful body sleep for the next twenty minutes.

When he woke up, he turned his head toward me. I stared straight into his eyes, not knowing what was about to happen. My heart quickened in anticipation.

"How long have I been asleep?"

"About an hour."

Dray smiled. "And how long have you been staring at me like that?"

I was at a loss but he wasn't waiting for an answer. He slowly reached for my hand as if it were the most natural thing to do and pulled me into him. I curled up beside him, and without another word Dray held my hand tight in his for the rest of the night. Obviously mathematics wasn't the only thing he was struggling with.

At first our relationship was based on the hottest sex of my young life. I mean we put it down! I'd had boyfriends over the years but the guys I met didn't last. When they weren't lying to me, they were coming up short in the bedroom. Not Dray. The boy could pound my ass into next week. In fact he was so skilled in this department that I would have sworn he'd been doing it his whole life. When asked pointedly if he had, Dray confessed to just one — and only one, he emphasized — drunken night with a basketball-playing buddy. Otherwise, he dated girls exclusively. I don't know why this admission comforted me, but knowing that he slept with women somehow put my mind at ease. I guess I felt they were somehow less competition than another guy.

But our sex life was not without its complications. After our first time together, I could see how guilty he felt the moment sex was over. He shut down suddenly, as if someone had thrown a switch. No longer the sweet-talking, smooth-as-silk man between the sheets, he turned dead serious, and in a tone more forceful than the situation called for, Dray made me promise to keep what we'd done a secret. He was especially terrified of his father finding out, believing the family would disown him. I thought this scenario a bit unlikely and said so. How would his father even hear about it, I asked. Rather than reassure him, my comment only inflamed his paranoia. Dray sat straight up and told me in no uncertain terms that if I so much as hinted to anyone that we'd gone to bed, he'd kick my ass. Not exactly my idea of pillow talk, but in that moment I saw that Dray was hurting more deeply than he was letting on. His threat felt overdone, a tough-guy pose meant to frighten me, when in reality the bewildered look on his face was all it would have taken for me to stand by his side. I stroked Dray's arm gently, vowing to keep his secret — now our secret. Nobody would ever find out, I promised, ever. All I asked in return was to continue seeing him.

Visibly relieved, Dray smiled his little-boy smile, then leaned over and kissed me gently on the lips. It was our first kiss. Although he didn't have to say it, I knew he would love me like I'd never been loved before.

The summer after his first year of college, Dray was picked by the Atlanta Hawks in the NBA draft, just as he and his dad had expected. This had been Dray's dream, and I was ecstatic over the news. Of course, I didn't know where the sudden shift left me. Our relationship had blossomed into a deep and loving one, and as much as I couldn't see Dray walking away from it, I couldn't see where I fit into his new life. While there had to be gay ballplayers, none of them were out of the closet. Dray wasn't about to become the first. Between the millions of dollars being thrown at him and the glow of celebrity that would accompany his career, our relationship would be scrutinized like never before. Something was going to have to give, and I feared it was going to be me.

I was therefore bowled over when Dray announced that I was moving to Atlanta with him. I asked how he planned to pull off our relationship right under the noses of the NBA brass, coaches, and agent. Apart from the NBA, I pointed out, there was also the media and all the fans. And let's not even get started with Dray's close-knit Southern family; surely he didn't think he could fool everyone. Dray smiled and told me not to worry. He had it all figured out, he said. I was hardly convinced, but I set aside my reservations. I was so grateful to be joining him after all that I didn't ask questions. Instead I threw my arms around his big shoulders and fought back tears of joy. It looked like the Hawks were getting two for the price of one.

ONE

Although I have two degrees, including an MBA from Georgia State University, I haven't worked a nine-to-five since I met Dray. When we first moved to Atlanta, I was kept busy furnishing his new condo and my town house, which were about ten minutes apart. Even though we spent a lot of time together, Dray thought it best that we have separate living quarters. I understood that. I even picked up a few clients for interior design work and then pursued my MBA at night but didn't tell Dray about it, because he made it clear he wanted me to be able to travel at a moment's notice to attend his road games.

Being Dray's love at times was like having a full-time job. I was responsible for purchasing most of his NBA wardrobe, which meant his suits, shirts, underwear, and ties. He bought his own jeans and sneakers. I set up his computer and iPod and made sure he had the latest electronic gadget. Life was easy and good. I had season tickets to the Hawks: I didn't miss one home game and attended as many road games as I could get to. I wouldn't call myself a huge basketball fan, but I loved going to the games to see what the wives, girlfriends, and groupies were wearing. At first I was envious that they got to show their love and support publicly, but later I felt sorry for many of them when Dray reminded me how much their husbands and boyfriends cheated on them when away on road games.

The first three years in Atlanta were like heaven.

Then she came along and everything changed.

The straight club scene in Atlanta bored me and the gay one didn't do much for me either. So I didn't mind when Dray went to the clubs and strip bars with his teammates. To me it was part of his job. But when one of his teammates suggested that I might be more than his interior designer/stylist, Dray went on a tear to find women. And trust me, the ladies were waiting.

At first he dated a couple of ghetto-fabulous sisters and some plain ghetto girls but got tired of them easily. I knew there was something different when he told me he'd met this young lady at a club in Miami after a road game there. He talked about how smart and beautiful she was and how much she knew about sports. Judi Ledbetter gave Dray the appearance of a socialite but sounded to me like a shrewd gold digger who gave good head, for a female, that is. I guess everybody is good at something.

I imagined her being like the ladies I sometimes saw in tony restaurants enjoying liquid lunches, and having flings with their well-built trainers. I had no proof this was the case with Judi, but it was my secret wish.

Before I knew it, she was doing some of the things Dray had depended on me to do for him, like buying his clothes, planning his vacations, and advising him on what products he should endorse. The difference between her advice and mine was that she did it with a feminine flair, whereas I always presented my advice as one of his bois telling him what was cool. I hadn't grown up in the lifestyle Dray and I were now living, but I'd done my homework to keep my head above water. I pored over style magazines like *GQ* and *Esquire*. I watched the Fine Living channel daily. I was constantly reading *InStyle* and *Architectural Digest*. My design background came in handy when I talked with the builders of Dray's condo about crown mold-ing, marble, and built-in bookshelves. When he built his first house it was I who suggested the indoor pool and the basketball and tennis courts.

As far as I was concerned, nothing seemed to change between Dray and me after he met Judi. I still saw him four to five times a week. But, unbeknownst to me, Dray had other plans that would cause things to change a bit. I showed no reaction when he announced that he was marrying Judi in what was to be one of the biggest weddings Miami's Star Island had ever seen. I'd seen it coming and told myself that I'd hold it together when he broke the news. I wanted to show him I could take care of myself. Needless to say, I didn't attend. Instead I spent the entire month of June touring Europe on Dray's dime so I didn't have to endure all the press attention their nuptials captured.

When he bought a mansion in Country Club Hills, my design input went unsolicited. Dray had to know my feelings were hurt, so he moved me out of my town house into a bigger house with a pool in Brookhaven and bought me a new Porsche. This didn't make me feel much better but I took his gifts anyway. If buying me a house and car made Dray happy, then that made me happy. Judi was none the wiser. I understood that Dray needed to be married or have a steady girlfriend to enhance his career with the Hawks and endorsers like Nike, Sean John, and Gatorade. I didn't like it but I understood. During his third year in the league, Dray was right behind Shaq, Kobe, and LeBron when it came to product endorsements. In his fourth year he was still a popular pitch man.

There was also the matter of his family, who had been pressuring him to marry. Dray came from a big family with three brothers and three sisters, who were now living in a slew of mansions Dray had built between Vicksburg and Jackson, Mississippi. His father, Henry, had quit his job as a construction worker and came to almost as many games as I attended, but I was never introduced to him or any of Dray's family. From what Dray told me, they were a close-knit bunch, but very country and conservative when it came to certain things. I translated that to mean that they wouldn't be too happy about our relationship.

My family, on the other hand, was a lot different. I'd been raised by a single mom in the small town of Burlington, North Carolina. My biological father left when I was six years old and I don't remember that much about him. Mama eventually started dating a guy who I called "Mr. Danny." I liked him, but he made Mama cry a lot and disappeared when he got Mama pregnant, and she found out he hadn't divorced his first wife. I loved Mama and would do anything in the world for her, because she made sure we always had food on the table and a roof over our heads.

As Dray made life more and more comfortable for me, I could take care of Mama and my fifteen-year-old sister, the beautiful Bella Lynn. With Dray's money I bought them a house in a nice neighborhood right outside Raleigh and paid the tuition for Bella, who was a budding ballet dancer at the North Carolina School of Ballet. I was already planning a sweet-sixteen party for her, which I hoped would rival some of the parties Bella and I watched on MTV.

My mother didn't know about Dray or where all the money came from, and just figured I was doing well with my career. I assumed she knew I was gay because Mama never asked me about girls or who I was dating, only stating one day very casually, "I just want you to be happy, baby. With whomever you choose."

About three months ago Dray said casually, after an evening of food, wine, and great sex, that I was moving to New Orleans. Just like that. He told me he'd found me a gorgeous two-story town house with a wrought-iron fence and a luscious garden and I was closing on it soon. When I asked why, he told me he asked the Atlanta Hawks for a trade because Judi didn't think pretty white girls were appreciated in Atlanta. She wanted to go to Denver or Los Angeles, but the Hawks got the last laugh by trading him to the New Orleans Hornets. Now Dray was on a team that, after Hurricane Katrina, didn't have a place to call home and spent two seasons in Oklahoma City.

So without further discussion I moved to New Orleans. A couple of days after Dray was traded, two burly Mexican guys showed up at my home to pack my belongings. Things were happening so fast, I almost let the movers pack my personal journals, which I protected like the Kentucky Fried Chicken recipe.

After a week in the New Orleans Ritz-Carlton, I moved into a refurbished town house in the middle of the famed French Quarter, now a resident of the rebuilding Crescent City.

I was getting ready to go out and explore my new neighborhood when the cell phone beeped, indicating I had a text message. It was the phone that only Dray called me on. "Got some free time. C u in 30."

I took off the jeans and polo shirt I was wearing and jumped in the shower for the second time that day. There were a few things I knew Dray liked without his ever telling me. He was a neat freak and personal hygiene was paramount. Dray always smelled good and kept his nails clipped and manicured. I knew he expected the same from me.

When I wore something he liked seeing me in, Dray would say, "You look nice in those jeans, AJ." I would make a mental note and buy several more.

After I got out of the shower, I covered my body with cocoa butter, then applied capsules of pure vitamin E to the few blemishes on my face. I looked at my abs and realized that they weren't as tight as they had been when I lived in Atlanta and worked out with a trainer four times a week. The one thing that I loved about New Orleans — the food — was already showing up on my lean but muscular five-foot-eight, 162-pound body with a booty like two soccer balls tied together. When I hired an assistant, the first task would be to have him find me a trainer so I could get back to the size I was when I competed in college gymnastics. I really didn't need a full-time assistant, but I'd heard a lot of young black men and kids in general were left unemployed in New Orleans after Katrina, so I made up my mind to hire someone who could help me adjust to the city and run errands for me. This would allow me to volunteer for one of the several organizations trying to bring the city back to its former self. I was really interested in Brad Pitt's Make It Right Foundation, which was building low-cost housing in the historic Ninth Ward.

Instead of putting my jeans back on, I threw on a pair of gray warm-ups that I knew Dray liked (without underwear) and a pink T-shirt. Now, it wasn't like Dray and I made love every time we saw each other; it had been two weeks since we'd put it down. I'd missed his smell and big hands caressing my head and ass.

I was still upstairs in my bedroom looking for a pair of sneakers when I heard the security bell. I looked at the alarm panel in the bedroom, which told me the back door had been opened. Dray had arrived. And not a moment too soon, I thought, as I quickly removed the greasy vitamin E from my face and replaced it with moisturizer.

"I needed that." Dray sighed as he playfully

31

pushed me off him.

I caught my breath and said, "You? I needed it more."

For a few moments, we lay in the bed in silence. I always loved these moments when the two of us would lie in bed in absolute solitude.

"What are you going to do with the rest of your day?" Dray asked.

"I'm going to meet a lady who heads up Brad Pitt's foundation here. I think they might be able to use some of my skills with the houses they are building."

"That's cool. AJ, you're a smart man. You'd be a big help to them."

"I hope so."

"So you like this place?" he asked, looking around my master suite.

"It's okay. There are still a few things I need to do."

"Like what?"

"I don't know if I like the color in this room. The yellow might be too pale," I said.

"It's calming," Dray said, snuggling closer to me, his arms tightening around my waist.

I quickly tried to pull back, hoping he hadn't noticed I'd picked up a few pounds.

"Don't do that," I said.

"What? Hold you? Or don't you think I noticed you put on a little weight?" He laughed. "AJ, I notice everything. But it's going to all the right places. And that's real talk, ba-bee."

"I'm going to hire a trainer," I said decisively. Even though we never talked about it, I knew Dray wanted me in top shape. I wanted to be in top shape too. It was one of those funny things about our relationship; we seldom said, "I need you to look good" or even "I love you," which I was sure he told Judi every day. Girls needed to hear that, but I told myself I didn't. All that mattered was that I knew Dray loved me, whether he actually told me or not. I just wish he kissed me more often.

"That's what's up," Dray continued. "I got a cousin who lives down here that used to train me. Mainly we just shot hoops. If you want I'll ask around and find you someone good."

"Don't worry about it, I'll find somebody. I know you're busy getting settled in your new house." Judi sprang to mind and I was hit by a wave of jealousy, but I didn't let Dray know. "How is it coming?"

"It's fine. Judi's like you, she's great at all that shit. When she's finished and goes back to Atlanta to close up the old house, I'll take you out to see the new one," he said. Dray's phone rang and he looked at it, then answered. I was lying so close to him that I knew from the look on his face that it was most likely his wife.

"What's up, babe? You miss me? Of course I miss you, J-Love." He smiled at me and winked, and then I heard him say, "If that's what you want, Judi, then get it. You know I'm not worried about how much it costs. Love you too, J-Love." J-Love? So that's what he called her. Dray may have thought it was cute, but it made me want to throw up.

He clicked off his phone and then looked at me and asked what we were saying before his phone interrupted our conversation.

I felt slighted but didn't want Dray to know, so I replied offhandedly, "I was just saying, you know, I'm here if you need me."

"I know you're here for me always. I 'preciate that, Aldridge Richardson," Dray said.

"I know," I answered softly, suddenly wishing I could hold back my tears and hear that every day of my life.

With Dray's birthday less than a week away, I still hadn't bought him anything and knew it was time to get busy. I'd thought that by coming to the Canal Place mall on a late Tuesday afternoon I'd practically have the place to myself. Even though I'd been in

New Orleans for only a short time, I knew better than to try this place on weekends. Anyone who says the city won't ever be the same after Katrina hasn't been to Canal Place on Saturday. I made that mistake my first weekend there. It was as jammed as Times Square on New Year's Eve. Still, weekdays also brought their fair share of shoppers, I discovered as I circled the parking garage for a space.

I'd seen an ad for Saks in the Sunday paper mentioning a special line of skin-care products for men that I used on Dray when we lived in Atlanta, and I figured that would be one of the gifts I could get him quickly and get back home in time to catch the Tyra Banks show.

I sometimes wondered what Dray would do if I weren't around — who'd buy him the hippest fashions and all the other odds and ends that kept him looking like a male model. Well, I guess Judi would look after him. She already did, from what I could see from the new shirts he'd been showing up in. More Ralph Lauren Purple Label and less Sean John. They weren't entirely his style and were usually the wrong colors for the time of year, but then I didn't expect she'd ever know him or his clothes the way I did. When I casually commented on the new shirts, Dray became self-conscious and tried to play it down. He told me he'd had them awhile, just hadn't worn them out before. I just smiled to myself and went along.

For a big pro basketball player who towered over any room he walked into, Dray sure could act the part of the little boy when it came to his birthday. I chalked this up to having parents who, despite their meager means, never tired of finding new ways to spoil their children. He loved surprises, loved me coming up with them. Didn't matter what. Dray liked not only expensive items like clothes or the latest gadgets, but silly stuff like the basketball-attired teddy bear I ordered from a company in Vermont. It wasn't about the price tag but the gesture. I will never forget the first time I bought the skin-care products and then set up the bathroom like it was a spa. I led him into the bathroom, sat him down, and gave him his first facial ever. He loved it.

Like most people who soak up attention, he wasn't always big on returning it. I don't mean I ever doubted his feelings for me; just the opposite — I always knew he loved me even if it was seldom expressed in so many words. Apart from the mind-blowing sex, there was Dray's romantic streak, which admittedly leaned toward the obvious and unimaginative, like store-bought flowers once on my birthday.

I have to say there were moments in the beginning where his need to be adored exhausted me. I thought, "Damn, how about throwing a bone my way. Make me feel special for a change." But most of the time I got a charge out of our dynamic. I loved taking care of him. I guess that came from my mom, who loved my sister and me more than anything in the world and made sure we knew it. A lifetime of unconditional love had to have rubbed off. I suppose this helps explain why I put up with Dray in departments that frustrated the hell out of me and would have sent any sane person bouncing out the door.

Opening the heavy double-glass doors of Saks Fifth Avenue, I stepped into the silver light of the fragrance department. The elegant room with its soft music, floor-to-ceiling mirrors, and smartly made-up women and men behind brightly lit sales counters looked like every other fragrance department I'd ever seen, but I felt an immediate sensation of well-being.

I'll admit it: I'm shameless when it comes to grooming. I could spend all day sampling colognes and lotions, testing one after another until the clerk finally would have to ask me to buy something or leave. Fortunately it never came to that. I'd promised myself that for once I wasn't going to get caught up. I was there to shop for Dray, and as soon as I had his gift I was done.

Passing the John Varvatos display of facial scrubs and skin cleansers, I was reminded how much Dray loved the Varvatos shirts I'd given him for Christmas. A tall, slim man wearing wire glasses greeted me as I approached the sales counter. There was no question the guy was gay, but the pink handkerchief tucked into his navy suit pocket was a classy touch that set him apart from the other queens working the floor. I asked to sample the aftershave lotion, which he opened for me. I dabbed a little onto the back of my palm and then lifted my hand to my nose, surprised by the pleasantly clean scent. The clerk insisted I try the matching fragrance. I took another sniff and for a moment was lost in thought at the picture of Dray curling up in bed with me while wearing his new cologne.

"Very nice," I said. "It's for a friend," I added, but wasn't sure why.

"Sure it is." The clerk grinned knowingly, then turned to his left to show me a gift box set that included the complete line of Varvatos skin-care products and scents.

I looked at him and wondered if he was trying to read me and if I was going to have to put him in his place.

Just as he handed me the box for inspection, two well-tailored women appeared directly in front of me on the other side of the counter. One was a blonde in an orange print blouse. She wore her hair up and was talking avidly to a younger woman, who I could tell right away was a less-polished carbon copy. The woman seemed to be listening so intently she might as well have been taking dictation. Right away they reminded me of the wives of ballplayers. In fact I only noticed the pair because the first blonde mentioned the Hornets in a voice so loud you could have heard her across a football field. I was used to that. Ballplayers' wives often dropped their husband's name as if it were a solid gold bar, which for them it almost was.

I was curious to know if she was connected to the Hornets, so I decided to listen to as much of their conversation as possible and bought time with the clerk by asking him to bring me other gift boxes of skin-care products. I handed him back the package, which he set on the glass shelf behind him. I pretended to browse the showcase.

As if on cue, the older blonde summoned the clerk. "Listen," she began in a manner so confrontational I couldn't tell whether she was about to ask a question or pimp-slap him in the face.

"Look, honey, it's my husband's birthday. Now he's not big on this stuff," she said with a sweep of her hand, "but he plays for the Hornets and I'm trying to teach him the importance of proper grooming. What would you suggest?"

The clerk graciously indicated the array of products in front of her, taking care to distinguish one from another. She was only half paying attention, however, as she brought her jeweled cell phone to her ear. As the clerk presented item after item, she kept talking on the phone.

"I won't know until he's home. They're in Philadelphia today, but he'll be back tomorrow. Next week is his birthday and I know he'll want to do something special. I might even have to give him some special sex. He can be such a chore." She shook her head impatiently at the last comment, though it could have just as easily been in response to the products being shown to her.

Then it hit me. I knew who she was. The floor might as well have opened from under me. How did I not put two and two together? Of course, who else could she be but Judi? I stood there dumbfounded, trying to decide my next move. Although there was no way she knew what I looked like — much less that I even existed — standing only a few feet from her so suddenly was like waking up with a cool puddle of water in your bed. Was it better to leave immediately or wait her out calmly and purchase my gift as if everything were normal?

I looked at her from the corner of my eye. She was not what I expected. She wasn't pretty or plain. Like many women she had learned that with money she could create the illusion of some sort of sorority-girl-pretty look with the right makeup or hairstyle. I guess the best way to describe her was as a slightly younger version of the lady who played Edie on *Desperate Housewives.* Thank God I wasn't competing with the character played by Eva Longoria, although with Tony Parker as the prize I might give it a shot.

Dray had dropped bits and pieces about Judi during pillow talk. I knew that Judi's father was loaded after selling his hedge fund for close to a billion dollars. A divorce from Judi's mother had taken care of half of that and Dray told me Judi's father had cut her off when she started dating Dray. He wasn't crazy about his only daughter shacking up with a black guy and told her she was now on her own. I knew she liked to shop and often left town for shopping sprees.

"How long is this going to take to gift wrap? I need to go to the jewelry counter and look at some rings. Maybe I'll use Drayton's credit card and buy you something, Amber. Just because I'm nice," Judi said, flashing a smile as phony as her hair color.

"And because you got a rich husband," the other woman said.

"So true. How lucky can a girl get? Rich daddy leaves, rich hubby appears magically out of thin air."

"I thought you said you met him at some black club in Miami."

"I did. Where else was I going to meet him, at the country club? I don't think so. Daddy's club was so sixties, Amber."

Finally I couldn't bear the pressure any longer, and as casually as I could, so as not to let Judi know how closely I was studying her, I stepped away from the counter. I made my way slowly for the door with my heart beating faster than my footsteps the

42

whole way.

It looked like Dray would get his favorite skin-care products for his birthday, even though they wouldn't be from me.

TWO

One of my three cell phones rang with an Atlanta number I didn't recognize, but I answered it anyway.

"Hello."

"What's up, bitch?" It was my good friend Maurice Wells, who lived in Jonesboro, Georgia, but had been raised in Selma, Alabama.

"Mo, what's good, boi?"

"Child, I still can't believe you upped and moved away from me. Now who am I gonna shop and gossip with? You know I don't trust these Atlanta sissies. Can't shit be going on in New Orleans."

"New Orleans is going to be all right," I said, as much to reassure myself as assure Maurice.

"You moved out of here so quick it was like the FBI came and moved you into the witness protection plan. Are you still hanging with old boi?"

44

"Yeah, we still hanging in there," I said.

Maurice was my closest gay male friend and one of the first people I had met when I'd moved to Atlanta. Still, he didn't know who "old boi" was. Maurice didn't know that Dray was one of the NBA's biggest superstars. It wasn't that I felt I couldn't trust Maurice. It was that I'd given Drayton my word that I would never tell anyone about our relationship.

I did share with Maurice that the man I was seeing was in the public eye, but I led him to believe that he was somebody in the music business. Maurice was always trying to guess Dray's identity and once he almost caught us when he showed up at my house a few minutes before Dray was expected to arrive. I panicked and went off, yelling at Maurice about how dare he come to my house unannounced. Maurice is no shrinking violet, and so he started cussing me back, asking me who in the fuck did I think I was.

Maurice left in a huff and it took several calls and a few gifts before the friendship was back on track. At least I never again had to worry about Maurice dropping in. We both learned our lesson after that incident.

Maurice and I met years ago at a B. Smith seminar at the Ritz-Carlton in Buckhead. He came up to me during the break and acted like he had known me for years. By the end of the seminar he was calling me "girl" and "bitch," two words I don't like, but I quickly realized he meant no harm. It was just the way he used them with his dramatic hand gestures when he talked.

He was also an interior decorator and event planner with a growing business. When I told him I did all my work for charity, he realized I wasn't a threat to him and seemed relieved. I never talked about him to Dray because Dray was always warning me about trusting people, especially gay men. But that didn't stop Maurice from quizzing me for clues about Dray.

There were times when I felt like I could trust Maurice because he shared so much of his personal life with me. He told me that when he was younger he was a crafty bitch with more scams than the Mafia. One day Maurice also told me, "I'd just as soon cut a sissy than speak to him. And I didn't do shit unless it was going to put some money in my purse or benefit me in some way. I leave the charity work for the white ladies."

I wouldn't have ever guessed that he was a recovering crack addict until he told me by saying, "I was the kind of functional drug addict that would wake up some days with my draws under the seat of my car."

"What would you do when that happened?"

"I'd ball them up and put them in the glove compartment of my car and go on to my meeting."

I looked at him to make sure he was serious and then both of us just burst out laughing. I adored him and knew I could trust him with my life. And he knew the same was true of me. With Maurice I could be myself, and felt like I did when I was writing in my journals as a young man trying to make sense of life.

"So did that phantom boyfriend move to New Orleans too?"

"Maybe."

"Are you sure he's not a drug dealer? Maybe he's a member of the Black Mafia."

"I wouldn't date a drug dealer," I snapped.

"So when are you coming back to Atlanta?"

"I don't know. I'm trying to get things settled here."

"Do I need to come down there and see what's up? I bet you could get trade down there for a Popeye's two-piece dinner. Extra spicy, of course." Maurice laughed.

"I'm scared of the bois down here. They are desperate and without much hope. What's going on in Atlanta?"

"Besides trying to run my potential new husband out of town?"

"Who's that?"

"Child, you know who I told you I was going to marry if I could ever meet him."

"I forgot." Maurice had crushes on all types of Atlanta men, popular and not. They always had one thing in common, besides being dark and masculine. They were all straight, or what were known as gay-for-pay guys.

"Mike Vick, bitch. They are trying to run that fine man out of town."

"Yeah, I heard that. Looks like he's in a lot of trouble, but we all know they going after him because he's a big name. I hope that shit's not true," I said. For a second I wondered what would happen to Dray if word ever got out about us but quickly realized that wasn't going to happen, because my lips were sealed and so were Dray's.

"I tell you what, bitch. If he goes to jail then I'm gonna throw a brick through a police station or smack a rich white lady so I can end up in the cell next to him."

"You think he's gonna get any time if he's convicted?"

"Oh, hell yeah. And I know you think I'm playing, but if I have to go to prison to meet Mike Vick, then it's going to be skip to my

Lou, my darling. I could also spruce the place up while I'm there like my girl Martha did when she was in the pen. I ain't scared of no jail."

"Did you send me the last of those boxes I left in your garage?" I asked.

"Oh, shit, I knew I'd forgotten something. I'll get them out tomorrow," Maurice said.

"That's cool. It's not stuff I can't live without, just personal papers I like to have close by." Maurice had saved the day by holding on to my belongings that I couldn't risk leaving unattended on a moving truck.

"Those boxes heavy as dried-up shit, but I'll get one of my bois to help me take them up to UPS or FedEx," Maurice said.

"Cool, and don't forget to let me know how much it costs."

I looked at the time and realized that it was almost three o'clock. One of the candidates interviewing for the position of my assistant was due any minute, so I told Maurice I needed to run.

"Okay, bitch. Now don't let me have to track your ass down again because it won't be pretty. You hear me?"

"I hear you, Mo. Take care of yourself."

"You do the same thang, baby."

THREE

There was a knock at my door and I figured it was my deli order of a bacon, egg, and cheese bagel along with some black coffee. When I opened the door, a humid August breeze slapped my face and there stood a young man with a wide grin. He was wearing a warm-up suit with a gym bag slung over his shoulders, but he didn't seem to have my breakfast.

"What's good?" he asked, walking into my home like the place had his name on the deed.

Stunned, I asked, "May I help you?"

"Are you . . ." He stopped and pulled a piece of paper from his pocket. He looked down at the slip, then up at me. "You Aldridge Richardson?"

"Yeah, that's me, but you still didn't answer my question."

"Cisco is my name. I'm your new trainer. I understand you have your own gym here.

Where is it, upstairs?" he asked, looking toward the staircase.

"Who hired you?"

"I do some freelance work for the Saints and I got a call from somebody in their office telling me that I was your new trainer. Got paid three months in advance and I thought to myself, 'Shit, I love these kinds of gigs.' You know, dealing with big ballers again." Cisco pulled the gym bag off his shoulder and laid it on the table where I kept my mail.

"You sure I'm the right person? I didn't ask anyone to call a trainer," I said, thinking I'd been called a lot of things, but never a big baller.

"This is the address they gave me. I was told to come straight over. Your name is the one I was given, so I guess you're my new client." Cisco smiled.

I hadn't yet had my breakfast so I figured this was as good a time as any to get started.

"Okay. I was waiting for some coffee but that'll have to wait. Would you like some water?" I asked. I figured Dray had tried to be helpful and hired me a trainer. It wasn't unlike him to do things like this without telling me, so I guessed I could trust this guy. I hadn't heard from Dray in about four days but this was typical of the ways he let me know he was thinking about me. He also did stuff like this to show that he was in charge, even though I was three years older.

"You know that caffeine shit ain't any good for you. And thanks, but I carry my own water with me."

I was getting ready to tell him that was cool when there was another knock at the door. Breakfast was here. I pulled a ten-dollar bill out of my wallet, opened the door, and paid a small Asian man the money. He handed me a brown paper bag that was warm from the coffee.

Cisco gave me the disapproving look that trainers seem to wear permanently as I placed the bag on the counter.

"That smells greasy," he said.

"I sure hope it is."

"You gonna eat that?" Cisco asked.

"Sure am."

"You know, you might not want to do that."

"Stop tripping. You don't even know what it is."

"I can smell the coffee and the bagel."

"Okay, let's get this over with," I said, pointing to the stairs. My bagel and coffee would have to wait.

"Lead the way."

When we reached the second floor, I gestured to the room at the end of the hall and told Cisco I would meet him there after I'd changed into some workout clothes.

I went into my dressing area and pulled out some black sweats, along with a white V-neck T-shirt. I put on some white ankle socks and my bright red Converse throwback sneakers. I walked down to the room I'd converted into a gym to find Cisco looking out the window. I noticed he'd removed his jacket. He was built like a football player, muscular and compact at about five-nine. He was wearing a white tank that hugged his upper body like spandex, and some baggy black warm-ups. His hair was done in little twists the length of Cheetos.

He pulled out one of the blue mats lying against the wall, placed it on the floor, and instructed me to lie on my back.

"I'm going to stretch you out real good," Cisco said, with what sounded like a double meaning.

I lay down and Cisco took my right leg and pushed it back into my chest until I grimaced in pain.

"That's you?" he asked.

I nodded my head to let him know he had indeed reached my pain threshold.

"How often do you work out?"

"I used to work out at least four times a

week. I've been slacking off since I moved down here."

"Where you moved from?"

"Atlanta."

"You ever play sports?"

"A little tennis, and I used to be a gymnast."

"That's what's up. I can tell you're real limber."

"Not like I used to be."

"What do you do? If you don't mind my asking," Cisco said. He moved behind me, pulling my arms behind my neck.

"I'm an interior designer," I said.

"Must be money in that because this joint is hooked up like a baller's pad. This looks like one of them houses on *MTV Cribs*. You seen that show?" I could feel his warm breath on the back of my neck with each of his words. I wanted to tell him if he thought this was something, he should have seen my house in Atlanta. Now that was something special.

"Yeah, I've seen it once or twice."

After a couple of sets of ab work, we moved to the weights. Within minutes sweat poured into my eyes as I lay on the bench. Cisco gave me a small white towel to dry my face.

As we went from station to station, Cisco was so close to me I noticed the faint smell of his soap-scented deodorant. We finished the workout with Cisco throwing a twelve-pound medicine ball to me over a hundred times. After all that I was so tired I thought I was going to tumble down the stairs. I needed some water and food. I suddenly remembered my cold breakfast bagel and hoped it would be the answer to my hunger.

"You all right with the water?" I asked.

"I'm straight."

While I was removing the cap from the bottle and taking several swigs, Cisco hit me with a barrage of questions: "You live here by yourself?" "You got a female?" "You think Mike Vick going to jail?"

"What do you think?" I asked, wondering which question he wanted me to answer first.

"About what?"

"Mike Vick. You think he's going to jail?"

"Shit, that would be some foul shit if he did. Kobe didn't do any time. And we talkin' 'bout some dogs. This ain't no white girl shit. Maybe if he had some white girls mud wrestling naked and him pissing on them he might have to give the man some time, but he ain't done no shit like that as far as I know." Cisco took a gulp of water from the clear gallon jug he was carrying with him.

"So what days are we going to work out?"

I asked.

"It's on you, playa. Tell me and I'm here."

"I like to start early in the morning. Is that a problem?"

"Like I said, my dude, it's on you. Say the time and I'm here."

"Is this all you do?"

"What do you mean?" he asked, slightly defensively.

"Is training your only job?"

"For right now. I was hoping to get into somebody's training camp before the season starts, but nobody has called yet."

"You play football?"

"I played at Southern down in Baton Rouge. A couple years ago I got invited to the Saints camp, but I got cut right at the end. I thought at least I'd make the practice squad. I played in the Arena League but that shit is lame. You have to play two positions and they don't pay shit. It's like peewee football for grown-ass men."

"What position do you play?"

"Safety. What is your favorite team?"

"The Dolphins," I said.

"What do you think about what they did to Culpepper?"

"I haven't been following them lately. What happened?"

"They waived that mofo's big ass. Most

likely he's happy as shit now that he's playing ball in a black town."

"Where is he playing now?"

"Oakland."

"I have to check that out. So let's work out
Monday, Tuesday. Take Wednesday off and
then pick it back up on Thursday and Friday. How does that sound?"

"I'm down. You want to start at seven?
That way you can be my first client and we
can just knock that shit out."

"Cool. What's your number?"

"Give me your cell phone and I'll punch it
in."

I handed Cisco my phone and he entered
his number, then threw the phone back to
me. He grabbed his gym bag, gave me some
ball-fisted dap, and was out the door.

Interesting guy, I thought, taking note of
his round ass poking out from the warm-
ups.

Yes, sir, that was definitely the body of a
football player — or a male stripper.

FOUR

I was enjoying the first sip of my café au lait at the popular New Orleans spot Café Du Monde when I heard a woman's voice calling in my direction.

"Are you going to use all that sugar?"

"No, not using it all," I said, passing her the light blue dish that held sugar and several kinds of artificial sweeteners.

"Thank you. I thought this was supposed to be a classy joint, and they can't even put sugar on every table."

I took another sip and nodded politely. I was just getting ready to taste my first bite of my beignet when she called out again.

"Why are you sitting over there by yourself?"

"I'm waiting for someone," I said, hoping this girl wasn't trying to hit on me so early in the morning. I was waiting to interview a candidate for the position of my assistant.

"Why don't I join you before he or she gets

here?" she offered. Before I could respond she had picked up her coffee and roll and plopped down in the chair facing me.

I was struck first by her boldness, then by how pretty she was, with her overdeveloped breasts bursting from her silky tank top. She had a soft face with dark sparkling eyes that radiated warmth and confidence.

"I'm Jade. Jade Galloway," she said, extending her hand.

"Nice to meet you, Jade. I'm Aldridge."

"That's a nice name. You got a last name?"

"Yeah, it's Richardson. Most people call me AJ," I said.

"That goes together and I like AJ," she said, blowing on her coffee with her full lips. I admired the way she was wearing her hair down, with a slight part amid an abundance of wavy black hair that looked part real, part weave. She didn't seem to be wearing any makeup on her smooth, tea-colored face, but she was so pretty it didn't matter.

"I'm glad you approve." I smiled.

"Are you from New Orleans?"

"No, I just moved here."

"Me too," she squealed with delight.

"Where are you from?" I felt obliged to ask out of courtesy. I looked at my watch and realized my appointment was running late. That wasn't a good sign for someone who intended to be my right hand.

"I moved here from Los Angeles, but I'm originally from St. Paul, Minnesota," Jade said.

"There aren't a lot of black people up there."

"You got that right. That's why I hauled ass right after I graduated from high school." She looked me directly in the eyes like she was sizing me up, and I couldn't tell if she was flirting with me.

"Did you go to college in Los Angeles?"

"No, I'm not the college type. I took a few acting classes and gave modeling a try like everyone else there." Jade moved her chair back a few inches from the table and crossed her slender legs. She was wearing a cute plaid, pleated skirt with a slight split that revealed her thigh. I thought to myself, if I was into girls this would be the type for me. She was pretty and I could tell that she had a wicked sense of humor.

"Have you been in any movies, or did you meet anybody famous when you were in Los Angeles?"

"I did a lot of extra work, and once Denzel Washington and his wife came in the restaurant where I was a hostess. I used to see a lot of rappers and hip-hoppers when I went to the clubs."

"I would think Los Angeles would be nice for a pretty girl like you. What brought you to New Orleans?"

"I got bigger fish to fry, and I need to catch my fish before everybody comes back here," she said with a grin.

"I heard that. Sounds like you got a plan."

"Miss Jade's always workin' on a plan."

"You think people will?" I asked.

"Will what?"

"Come back to New Orleans."

"I think so, but not until after the white folks buy all the real estate so they can sell and rent it back to poor black people for more than it's worth."

For someone who had only completed high school, Jade sounded like she had a good head on her shoulders, even if she looked like the sports groupies who hung outside the locker room after games or in hotel lobbies.

"Have you found a job here?" I asked.

"No. You got one for me?" she said, laughing.

"I don't think so." I finally took a bite of my sweet, doughy breakfast treat covered with powdered sugar.

"You found a job yet?"

"Who said I was looking for a job?" I asked.

"If you don't have a job, why are you sitting in this café at ten o'clock in the morning? Are you independently wealthy? That must be nice," she said.

"I don't have it like that," I said, fibbing a bit.

"What do you do?"

I wiped the powdered sugar from my mouth. "I'm an interior designer." The truth was that I was a kept man who did a little charity work on the side, but that would take too much explaining. Besides, I didn't like the term "kept." I knew that I could take care of myself if I had to.

"That sounds like fun."

"I enjoy it," I said.

"Where do you live?"

"I have a place in the Quarter."

"You must be a big baller, staying in the Quarter. I'm living in an SRO hotel but I'm going to get me a place once I get a job and a car."

"You got any leads?"

"Yeah, I do. I'm on my way for a second interview as a cocktail waitress at the casino. I heard that you make good tips and I figure it will do until I get the job I came here for. I got some other skills." Jade smiled mischievously.

"You mind sharing with me?" I smiled back. Right as she was getting ready to respond, my cell phone rang and I asked Jade to excuse me.

"Hello?"

"Mr. Richardson, this is Doyle Johnson. I was going to meet you at ten A.M."

"Yeah, Doyle. I'm waiting for you," I said, looking at my watch. It was now close to 10:30.

"Sorry, but I've been waiting for the bus for over an hour. These assholes haven't showed up yet."

"You don't have a car? What about a cab?"

"I don't have a car and I can't afford a cab even if I could get one to come to my neighborhood."

"Would you like to reschedule?" I asked politely. In my mind I knew that Doyle had just lost his chance to be my assistant, but I didn't want to tell him that now. I really didn't need an assistant anyway, and it would just be another person for Dray to worry about finding out about the two of us.

"Sure."

"Okay, I'll call you when I have some more time. Have a nice day." I clicked off my phone and returned my attention to Jade. "Now where were we?"

"I was going to tell you about the job I really came here to get, and my special skills."

"Oh, yeah. What job and skills?"

63

"You're going to laugh," Jade warned.

"No, I won't." I pulled a small piece from my beignet and popped it in my mouth.

"You might think I'm crazy," Jade said, looking bashful all of a sudden.

"I promise I won't," I assured her.

"Okay, you have a nice face and I think I can trust you."

I leaned in closer to her and gave her an "Okay, tell me" look.

"Which do you want to know first?"

"Tell me about your special skills."

"Oh, that's easy. I'm psychic, and I'm pretty sure we're meeting for a reason."

"You think so?"

"Yeah, I'm pretty sure I'm gonna have something to do with your love life."

"Who said I have a love life?"

"You do."

"So how are you going to do that?"

"I don't know yet."

"Okay, I can live with that. So tell me about this big job you came here for."

She took a deep breath before releasing her big announcement. "I came here to be Mrs. Reggie Bush."

"You mean the football star?"

"Yep, that would be him."

"Do you know him?"

"Not yet," Jade said, intimating that it was

only a matter of time.

"Isn't he dating that Kardashian girl?"

"That big-booty gold digger," Jade said, waving her hand in a dismissive gesture. "Baby, please."

"Do you have a plan?" I asked, intrigued by my new friend. I'd heard of girls moving to a city to meet local celebrities, especially football and basketball players, but I'd never actually met one. Dray called them jock sniffers or cleat chasers.

"I do, but I'm keeping that to myself. Oh, shit," she said, with a glance at the huge clock on the wall. "If I don't leave now, I'm going to be late for my interview." Jade grabbed her fake Louis Vuitton bag, rose from the table, and took a final swig of her coffee.

"You gonna leave me hanging?"

"We'll see each other again," she said, and just like that she darted out of the café and into the steamy New Orleans morning.

In spite of the heat, I took a leisurely stroll through the Quarter. By the time I got home, I was soaking wet from the humidity. I cooled down with a shower, and when I got out I could hear one of my cell phones ringing.

"Hello?"

"Hey, baby."

"Mama, where are you calling me from? The number came up as private."

"I'm at the department store. I was looking for a dress for Bella's sweet-sixteen party and I wanted to know if I had a limit," Mama asked. I could tell she was clearly hoping there wasn't one.

"No, you don't have a limit," I said. This was one of the more enjoyable fringe benefits of having a rich boyfriend, being able to take care of my mother and little sister. But even if I didn't have Dray, I still would be able to make a decent living on my own. Thank God for my degrees.

"Okay, because I see this cute black lace dress with a pink underlining and they have them in both Bella's and my size."

"Does she still wear a zero?" I asked playfully.

"Yes, that dancing keeps that girl rail thin."

"I was thinking about surprising her in the next couple of days. They have a little more work to do on my place and so I was thinking about getting out of this hot city."

"It's hot up here in Raleigh too, baby. I think it's hot everywhere."

"Thank God for central air," I said.

"But come on. We'd love to see you and get to hug that neck of yours." Just as I was getting ready to tell her I was coming up soon, the phone that Dray called me on rang.

"Hold on a second, Mama."

"Okay, baby."

I picked up the other phone and clicked it on. "Hello?"

"What's up, AJ?"

"Hey, Dray. What up?"

"Check the flights to Los Angeles and get the first thing you can."

"What?"

"I'm in Los Angeles working a camp with some of the Lakers players. They hooked me up with a nice suite in Beverly Hills." Then, in the low sexy voice he used when he wanted me, Dray said, "It will give me some time to give you da business." I'd not heard from Dray all week and the thought of a few days alone with him got me excited just thinking about it. "Give me da business" was the term Dray used for really putting it down in the bedroom.

"When?"

"Today."

"Oh, I don't know if I can do that," I said.

"Why not?"

"I was thinking about going to see my family."

"You see them all the time. Now do what I said, Mr. Richardson, and get that fine ass of yours on a plane ASAP."

"But, Dray, I also have my second meeting with the foundation this afternoon. They were excited to hear from me and think that I can help them."

"That's all well and good, AJ, but I'm sure you can reschedule the meeting for after you get back. I really need to see you. Don't you know what tomorrow is?"

"What?"

"My birthday, silly. Even though you already gave me one of my birthday presents, I know you got something else cooking."

"You think so?" I asked. I had somehow forgotten tomorrow was his birthday, even though I had spent days buying gifts for him, including the new iPhone I knew he wanted. It wasn't like he couldn't afford one on his own; he just liked it when I bought it for him. It didn't matter that it was his money to start with.

"Okay," I said, feeling I was about to let down my mother and my sister too. "Let me get on the computer and check the airlines." I resigned myself to the fact that I was on my way to Los Angeles, and it really didn't matter to Dray how much I wanted to see my family.

"Call me before you take off."

"Will do."

I clicked off the phone and put the other

one with my mother to my ear.

"Sorry, Mama."

"Is everything all right?"

"Sure. But it looks like I won't be able to make it this weekend."

"Why?" she asked, the disappointment clear in her voice.

"One of my clients needs me to fly to Los Angeles to check on some furniture. Duty calls," I said, hating that I was lying to my mother.

"Well, maybe next week. I'll tape Bella's performance. AJ, Bella is really getting good with this dancing. She is thinking about running in that teen pageant, and if she does you can't miss that," Mama said. "She'll never forgive you if you don't show up for that."

"I will. Got to run, Mama. I love you."

"Love you too, baby. Don't work too hard."

FIVE

A little after two A.M. I arrived at LAX. I hadn't checked my luggage, so I went straight to the limo section and saw a big, buff blond guy with sunglasses holding up a sign with my last name on it. When I walked up to him and told him I was Mr. Richardson, he looked startled. As if he doubted I was his real passenger, he asked me where I was going.

"To the Peninsula Hotel in Beverly Hills," I said with irritation.

"Then you got the right guy," he answered, sounding slightly friendlier than before.

I could tell he was the talkative type, so when we got into the car I wanted to say I was tired and didn't feel like talking. He could go back to being his snotty self. But I didn't.

"Where you from?"

"North Carolina."

"Is that where you came from today?"

"No," I said, hoping he would get the clue from my short answers.

"Where did you start your day?"

"New Orleans."

"How is it there now?"

"Better."

"Do you think it will ever be the same?"

"I hope so."

"How long have you lived there?"

"Not long."

"Do you come to Los Angeles much?"

"No."

"You here on business or pleasure?"

"Both."

"The hotel you're staying at is real nice. A lot of celebrities and ball players stay there. Do you play ball?"

"No," I answered. I wanted to respond, Do I look like a ball player at five-foot-eight?

"What type of business you in?"

"Interior design."

"Okay. I'll let you rest. You must be tired."

Finally, I thought, as I repositioned myself in the back of the limo. Just as I got comfortable and was about to kick off my shoes, I heard his voice again.

"Well, here we are. I'm going to give you my card in case you need a driver while you're out here. Do you need help with your luggage?"

"Thanks, but I don't have much. Just one bag. I can make it."

"I guess you won't be out here long."

"No, not long," I said, stepping out into the cool morning air. Thank God it wasn't as hot as it had been in New Orleans.

The opulent hotel lobby was empty and quiet. I walked up to the marble front desk where the night clerk looked busy on the computer.

"Excuse me," I said.

"Yes, sir, how can I help you?" She smiled.

"Are you holding a key for an Aldridge Richardson?"

"Let me check."

After a few minutes she said, "Yes, here we go. Your party is in villa eight. All you need to do is go out the double doors around the corner. There will be signs. Do you need help with your luggage?"

"No, thanks, I'm fine."

She handed me the pass key and I nodded thank you.

I walked around the corner and through the double doors and followed the sign that led to villas 7 to 12. I got excited at the thought of sleeping next to Dray. We didn't get many chances to do that since he'd gotten married. When I reached number 8 I slowly climbed the stairs and opened the door.

The living room was decorated with traditional furnishing and a fireplace was roaring while soft music played, but there was no sign of Dray. I noticed a half-finished bottle of champagne and some chocolate-covered strawberries on the bar. I walked over and saw a "welcome to the hotel" note addressed to Dray and poured myself some champagne. It was sweet and not flat, leading me to guess it hadn't been open long.

I grabbed my products bag from my suitcase, went into the bathroom, and brushed my teeth and took off my clothes, leaving my T-shirt and underwear on the floor. Then I walked into the large master bedroom. There I found Dray sprawled out on the bed, his back turned toward me. He was sound asleep. I crawled into the king-sized bed as quietly as I could and began to look for the remote so that I could turn off the television.

Just as I settled into my spot in bed, I felt Dray's huge hands wrap around my waist and pull me close to him in the spoon position. Since he wasn't usually a cuddler, I was going to enjoy this.

"You made it," he said, kissing me on my ears and neck. Dray wasn't wearing underwear and the warmth of his body soothed me. "I'm so glad you're here, AJ. You're not mad at me, are you?"

"For what?" I asked.

"Making you cancel your meeting and your trip to see your family."

"No, I'm cool. I called the foundation and they said I could come in when I get back. I'll see Mama and Bella another weekend."

"Cool, boi."

"Oh, I forgot. Happy birthday, Dray."

He looked at the clock and then back at me and said, "Yeah, it is my birthday. Where are my gifts?" He smiled expectantly.

"Why don't we wait until tomorrow?"

"That's cool. I already know I'm getting an iPhone."

"You do? How do you know that?"

"Because I know you and I know you know I love gadgets."

"Maybe your wife will get you one," I said, half teasingly.

"No, she already gave me my gifts before I came out here. She bought me a watch, some shirts, and that skin-care stuff you give me facials with."

I'd debated whether to tell Dray I'd run into Judi. I didn't want to trip him out but at the same time I wanted him to know. Since he brought it up, I went ahead.

"I know," I said quietly.

"How do you know that?"

"I saw her buy it."

"You did?" Suddenly he was wide awake.

"Yeah, she was with some other lady and I was in the store getting ready to buy you that skin-care package. But Judi beat me to the punch. I felt kinda silly."

"Why, baby boi?"

"I don't know. I just did. But don't worry. I didn't say anything to her and avoided eye contact."

"AJ, you could have gotten it for me and just kept it at your house. Do you think she saw you?"

"She didn't even look in my direction."

"I'm surprised she didn't remember you from the party," Dray said.

"What party?"

"Remember the one the Hawks owner gave and you came? She was there. I know you saw her."

"Oh yeah, but remember you didn't introduce us," I teased.

"I didn't think you wanted to meet her."

"That was cool. So how was camp today?"

"It was cool, but they are working my ass off. Still need to get that free-throw mojo working again."

"It will happen, babe. You'll get it back," I said, stroking his chest.

"You ready for da business?"

"Yes, babe."

"So when do I get my birthday kiss?"

"Now, and as many as you want." I kissed Dray deeply and he held me tightly. This was going to be a great couple of days, I thought, suddenly very happy Dray had made me cancel my trip home.

Then he nudged his head into my neck and the next thing I heard was Dray's snoring. Da business would have to wait for another night.

When I woke up, Dray had already left for camp. There was a note in the bathroom telling me he'd be back around six and to get ready for a special night. In anticipation I did the Hollywood wives thing, big time.

The weather in Beverly Hills was magazine-cover perfect, with a warm breeze. I had breakfast on the terrace by the pool and was going to call the chatty limo driver to take me shopping, but the hotel concierge offered me their driver. I was taken to Rodeo Drive, where I went into several trendy shops, including my favorite, Gucci. After a couple of hours, I purchased a pair of sheer black briefs with a matching undershirt that I knew would blow some blood to Dray's dick later that evening. I bought Dray five Italian shirts we couldn't get in New Orleans and a couple of knit shirts to wear with jeans. I even found a couple of pairs of size-thirteen sneakers I knew he didn't own. I loved buying clothes for him, even though technically I was spending his money. It made me feel even closer to him.

After a late lunch with two glasses of wine at a steakhouse on Robertson Boulevard, I called the driver to come and take me back to the hotel. I had to get ready for my special evening with Dray.

When I got back to the hotel, the bellman took my shopping bags and promised to send them to the villa. I walked through the lobby empty-handed, noticing several women, both black and white, enjoying high tea in front of a huge fireplace.

I reached the villa and was a little surprised to find the DO NOT DISTURB light on, but figured it was a mistake. I placed my key in the slot but instead of the green light going off, a faint yellow light in the middle flashed. I double-checked to make sure that I was at villa 8 and then I tried it again, but got the same result.

Maybe one of my credit cards had demagnetized the card key when I put it in my wallet. I went back to the lobby to get another key.

A petite desk clerk with brunette hair wound into a tight bun smiled from behind the front desk.

"Something is wrong with my key," I said, handing her the card.

"Sorry about that, sir. What's your room number?"

"I'm in villa eight."

"May I see some form of identification?"

"Sure." I pulled out my driver's license.

She looked at it and then punched in a few keys on her computer. Something was wrong. She looked puzzled and said, "Sorry, sir, but are you sure you're in villa eight?"

"Yes, I am sure," I answered with confidence.

"Then there must be some mistake. This villa is in the name of Mr. and Mrs. Drayton Jones. I know that's right — I checked in Mr. Jones yesterday and gave a key to his wife a few hours ago. I remember him because he was so tall."

"His wife? Are you sure?"

"Absolutely. We chatted about the huge pink diamond she was wearing. She told me it was a gift from her husband and that they were out here celebrating some big news and her husband's birthday. She was so happy and excited."

I was at a loss for words and for a moment just stood there in silence. At first I was embarrassed. I must have looked like a fool trying to get in a room I obviously now didn't belong in. Then I got mad wondering what Judi's ass was doing out here. How could Dray do this to me?

Did he know about this? And if so, what kind of sick game was he playing with me? I was beginning to wonder just how long I could play this secret-lover bullshit now that Judi was in the picture. It was okay when I was the only one and we were just keeping our secret from his teammates.

Just as I was about to ask if there were any vacancies, I noticed the bellman out of the side of my eye. He had placed my packages on a cart and was getting ready to take them to the villa.

"Excuse me. Are those going to villa eight?"

He looked at the claim tags and said, "Yes, sir. These are for Mr. Richardson."

"I'm Mr. Richardson. I might be changing rooms. Can you just hold them for a second?"

"Yes, sir."

I asked the desk clerk for a new room, but after tapping on her computer for what seemed like an eternity, she looked up and said flatly, "I'm sorry, Mr. Richardson, but we're completely sold out."

"Are you serious?"

"Yes, sir. We are completely full. If you like I can check some other hotels. The Beverly Hilton right nearby might have rooms available. Would you like me to check?"

I wanted to strangle Dray for sticking me in this mess. Here I was, miles from home, looking like a country fool.

"Give me a few minutes." I went into the dimly lit bar off the lobby and pulled out my phone. I didn't have any new messages. Dray hadn't called so I dialed his number. It went straight to voice mail, which meant he was either on the line or it was shut off. I bet he had shut it off the minute Judi arrived. So I sent him a text, telling him to call me immediately. I sat down at the bar and ordered a club soda while I waited.

Thirty minutes later, only my thirst had been quenched, so I called again. No answer. I sent another text. Minutes passed and still nothing. What was I going to do? Heading to the villa wasn't an option. Making a scene wasn't the way I rolled and Dray knew that. I would never serve up a confrontation in front of his wife. I didn't ever let on when I was jealous of Judi. I knew I couldn't beat her if I did the same dumb things Dray told me Judi sometimes did to get his attention, like crying or throwing a tactless tantrum.

The bartender approached. "Would you like another club soda or maybe something stronger? You look stressed."

"What?" I was so lost in my thoughts I hadn't noticed him.

"Would you like another drink?"

"No, I'm fine."

"Okay, just let me know."

"I will. Thanks."

I sat there feeling completely alone, knowing no one and not having a clue what to do next. What had Dray done with the few items of clothing I'd brought for the trip? Would I wait for Dray's call or just take my ass back to New Orleans?

Just as I walked out of the bar, my cell phone rang. Maybe this was Dray and if it was, I was ready to let him have it.

"Hello," I said, more as a challenge than a greeting.

"Dude, I'm sorry 'bout this. I had no idea she was coming," Dray whispered in a low and serious voice.

"What the fuck is going on?"

"It ain't happening. You need to go back to New Orleans."

"What?" I yelled. An elderly white couple turned in my direction, but I didn't give a damn who heard me. "Like that I'm supposed to turn around and leave just because

81

your wife shows up?"

"Look, AJ, stop trippin' and do like I said. I'll make this up to you. I gotta run. She's just turned off the shower."

Click.

What the fuck?

Three hours later I boarded a flight to New Orleans, having cleared standby with a coach seat at the last minute. No first-class ticket and no magical night with Dray. I was pissed as fuck and was going to let Dray know when I saw him next.

The plane was packed with passengers, including what looked like fifty high school cheerleaders returning from some sort of competition. When I finally reached my row toward the back of the plane, I realized I had a middle seat. Sitting by the window was a young black guy shaking his head with an iPod in his hand. He didn't pay any attention as I sat down.

Just as the plane was beginning to taxi, a white girl who sorta favored Dray's wife sat down right next to me. She smiled with teeth so white she could have lit up a lighthouse. After she had placed her bags in the overhead compartment and under the seat, she let out a loud sigh. "Looks like we got a full flight."

I didn't respond.

"So how was your day?" she asked with the concern of a former high school cheerleader.

Wrong question, lady.

"Bitch, don't ask me shit," I snapped, and I placed the airline-issued earphones into my ears, slipped on my dark shades, and closed my eyes.

SIX

Sometimes I don't know if I chose the life I lead or if it chose me. No, I don't mean the age-old question about whether or not one picks one's sexual orientation (I know I was born this way), because I've always been comfortable with the skin I'm in. I'm talking about the situation I'm in with Dray. Why couldn't I have picked someone who wanted only to be with me? Why didn't I meet a man who was man enough to admit who he really was? Could I really be ashamed of being gay but telling myself otherwise?

Thoughts like these have been running through my head lately. I've been back in New Orleans four days and still no word from Dray. Nothing. No calls, texts, or e-mails. When he doesn't reach out to me like this, I don't stalk him down, no matter how mad he makes me. Besides knowing that I'll keep my word about maintaining our secrecy, he needs to know he's not the center of my world. I'm so used to my situation that I can't get mad anymore. If I really didn't like it, I would do something about it. But here's what I do like: a healthy bank account and a partner who can lay the pipe down. Now that's real talk. Who was I kidding? I would be with Dray if he drove a bus or collected trash. I loved this man and it was going to take more than a wife for me to give him up completely.

At times like this, I wish that Dray and I were still back in college when we could be together whenever we wanted. I longed for the days when I had the upper hand and Dray needed me more than I needed him. Back then the two of us didn't have two nickels to rub together, but we were happy. At least I thought we were.

Dray used to tell me all the time about the wonderful places we would live and the cities we would visit once he made it to the pros, but I didn't really believe him. I figured the moment he got that first check from his agent it would be "See you, Aldridge." But I kept my word and never said anything about our relationship to anyone. Dray greatly valued that I was so loyal to him and so he kept his promises — at least he did back then.

Tomorrow I have my second workout with Cisco and I'm looking forward to it. Anything to get my mind off Dray. I've been lazy

the last couple of days, feeling sorry for myself and eating a lot of comfort food like
fried chicken and pasta.

But I've got to get over myself quickly.
Who is going to feel sorry for me if I've got
a fat ass? I know the difference between *phat*
and *fat*.

"Come on, Aldridge, you can do this," Cisco
said, pushing me to complete the last set of
arm curls. I was sweating like a fat man in a
plastic suit.

"How many more?" I asked, almost
breathless.

"Last five. Come on. Five . . . four . . . three
. . . two . . . one. Okay, I'll take it," Cisco said,
taking the fifteen-pound weights from my
hands. "Good job."

"Man, you trying to kill me." I looked
around the room for the bottle of water.

"Just doing my job." Cisco smiled.

I located the tall bottle and drank until it
was empty. The flat-screen television hanging from the wall showed Michael Vick
dressed in a nice blue suit entering a court-
room surrounded by reporters.

"I think he's going to jail." When I lived in
Atlanta, what a big fan I was of that handsome quarterback until I met Warrick Dunn,
another Falcons player who was really doing

something in the community. Every year Warrick built brand-new homes for single moms in the Atlanta area. I was so impressed with his charity that I called his foundation and offered my services gratis. I'm sure Vick had a foundation as well, even though I'd never heard of it. After some persuading I had convinced Dray to start two foundations, one to give back to the community he played for and the other in his hometown in Mississippi. It didn't take much to make Dray realize the importance of a positive community image for a highly paid athlete, especially one with a secret boyfriend on the side.

"Who, Vick? They gonna make an example out of that idiot," Cisco said.

"I heard he's got a great lawyer."

"Ain't gonna make a bit of difference 'cause when the man wants to get a brotha, they get it done."

"You think he'll play again?" I asked as I positioned myself on the mat to begin a series of situps.

"Yeah, he'll play, but I bet it won't be for the Falcons. They're going to drop his ass. I can't believe he messed up his chance to be the shit of the league over some fucking pit bulls," Cisco said as we finished the set.

"Are you going to try out again for

the NFL?"

"It ain't up to me, because if it was, I sure as hell wouldn't have my ass back in this shit of a city trying to get a steady gig," Cisco said with disgust. He pulled a plastic water bottle from his green gym bag.

"I thought you liked New Orleans."

"What's to like? I was born here. I just knew playing football was going to be my way out of this mutherfucker. Niggas like me would do anything to play in the league and the ones who have the chance to play are fuckin' it up for everybody else. If they would let me in the league I'd be a model citizen. They would never have to worry 'bout me doing some dumb shit."

"Where would you want to live?"

"Miami or the ATL."

"Atlanta's nice," I said.

"Is that where you were raised?"

"No, I grew up in North Carolina."

"What was that like?"

"It was cool," I said. I heard one of my cell phones on the table ring. I looked at the screen and saw that it was Dray calling. I didn't answer because I was still pissed off at what had happened in Los Angeles. Now that he'd finally decided to call, he'd have to wait for me to get back to him.

"Are there a lot of black folks in North

Carolina?"

"Some," I said. Then I heard my other cell phone ring. I looked down and there was Dray's name flashing on the screen. I guess he must be missing me bad right about now. I wasn't going to play it slow and easy.

"Looks like someone is really trying to reach you," he said, nodding to the phone.

"Just a friend."

"Well, AJ, I'm gonna bounce. You did well today. We'll step it up a little bit tomorrow."

"We working out tomorrow?"

"Yeah, like you said, two days on, take off a day to let your body heal, and then we hit two days in a row. That's the schedule I try to keep all my clients on."

"Cool. I'll see you tomorrow," I said as I gave Cisco some dap and watched him walk out of the room to the sound of my phone ringing again.

It felt good to be needed.

A flash of lightning and a clap of thunder that sounded like a slap against naked skin woke me early the next morning. I sat up in bed, allowing my eyes to adjust to the darkness, when I heard a voice.

"Do I have to come all the way over here to talk to you? So why haven't you returned my calls, Aldridge?" Dray was standing a few feet from my bed, removing his V-neck T-shirt. His presence damn near gave me a heart attack. He caught me completely off guard, so much so that for a second I forgot how angry at him I was.

"I got the messages too late," I lied. "I was going to call you first thing in the morning."

"Did you miss me?" He sat on the edge of my bed and removed his sneakers and socks. Then he stood up and dropped his warm-ups to the floor. Down came his boxers, which he kicked across the room.

"Of course I missed you." The rage I felt in the Los Angeles hotel suddenly felt like a lifetime ago.

"I'm sorry about spoiling our trip, AJ. I really am. I didn't know she was coming. I had no idea Judi was going to show up. I wanted to spend my birthday with you."

"I know."

"So you forgive me?"

"You know I do."

Dray walked over to my music system and turned on the iPod. Suddenly Ne-Yo's voice filled the bedroom. Dray was breathtaking to look at walking around the room, nude with his ten and a half inches of Mississippi pride dangling. I couldn't take my eyes off his muscled thighs, narrow hips, and plump, muscular ass.

He crawled into the bed and began kissing me. Dray's kisses were sometimes so deep it felt like he was plowing into me. I remember when we first started messing around he wouldn't kiss my lips, only my forehead and sometimes my neck. Boy, how things had changed. He climbed on top of me and began to grind his pelvis against mine. The pleasure I felt from his kissing only intensified.

As Dray removed my underwear, I noticed a dreamy smile softening his face.

"I want you so bad, boi. You know that?"

"I want you too."

"Show me."

"How?"

"You know what I like."

"You like my sex, huh."

"That's not all I like."

"Really? What else do you like about me?"

"That you're handsome. Smart. And I know you really care about me," Dray said as I stared into his soulful eyes.

"How much do you care about me?"

"Come on, AJ, you know how I feel about you."

"Tell me."

Dray looked away for a moment and then smiled at me and said, "I love you, boi."

"You really mean that?"

"You know I do. I don't know how I could

make it without you."

"You'd survive," I said.

"Barely. But why are we talking about serious shit? I thought I was handling da business," Dray said as he got back on top of me.

I playfully pushed him off me, and reversed positions so that I was now on top of him, kissing his chest. I moved my tongue down his body until I reached his groin area and then buried my face into his lap, taking in every inch of Dray's Mississippi pride.

When I woke up later that morning, a huge smile crossed my face. Dray was still lying in my bed, staring at me and gently rubbing his huge hands across my forehead. I had just assumed he would go home after I went to sleep. I needed to call Cisco and change my training session.

"So sleepyhead finally wakes up," Dray said.

"What are you doing here?" I said, sitting up in the bed.

"What, you expecting your other boyfriend?" Dray teased.

"Now, you know he comes during the day when we know you're at practice."

"Just don't let me catch you with that nigga."

"Who said he was black?" I said as I got

ready to leave the bed, only to be pulled back by Dray grabbing the bottom of my white T-shirt.

"Come on, Dray, let me go. I got to pee," I pleaded.

"Not until you give me a kiss."

I turned around and quickly gave him a peck on the lips and then raced to the bathroom. I tried to call Cisco but got his voice mail, so I left a message. When I came back some ten minutes later, after making sure I'd brushed and flossed my teeth, combed my hair, washed my face, and moisturized my body, Dray wasn't there. I called out his name but he didn't answer. I went down the stairs and when I got halfway down I could smell food. Wonderful food.

I walked into the kitchen and there was Dray in his boxers and T-shirt, managing three different pots and pans on the stove top.

"I hope you're hungry, baby, because I sure am."

"What are you doing?"

"What does it look like I'm doing? I'm cooking us breakfast."

"Don't you have to get to practice? Or go home? Is Judi going to be looking for you?"

"I got that covered, babe. No practice this morning and Judi is down in Miami doing some furniture shopping. You got me all day."

"When is the last time you cooked for me?" I asked. It had been so long that I'd forgotten what a great cook he was. When we started dating in college, he used to make hamburgers and homemade potato chips and then pour blue cheese over them. I loved the fattening snack. I thought for a quick moment about Judi being down in Miami spending Dray's money, but I wasn't going to let something I couldn't control ruin my day.

"It's been a while. That's why I'm making your breakfast favorites." Gesturing from one pan to the next, he said, "We got scrambled eggs with onions and cheddar cheese, grits, honey-glazed bacon, and some store-bought biscuits. It looks like you're out of blueberry jam but I found some strawberry."

"It smells great."

"What would you like to drink?"

"Some coffee."

"That's not good for you, baby. How about some cranberry juice?"

"So I can't have coffee?"

"Cranberry juice."

"Why?"

"Because it's better for you."

"So you know what's best for me," I teased.

"I think I do. Hey, I been thinking that maybe we ought to change our password," Dray said.

"Why?" Ever since Dray had gotten married, we had a password that only the two of us knew. If I got a text or e-mail that seemed strange or didn't sound like Dray, I would ask for the password, and he did the same with me. We changed them every now and then so as not to get caught with some of the sexy messages we sometimes left for each other.

"Just makes sense. I know women and I know Judi. She usually does her best snooping when she's been away. I erase all my texts and e-mails but you never know. I still have two cell phones she doesn't know about."

Our current password, which we've had since we've been together, is "speed bike." Dray thought of it when he came up with the bright idea in Atlanta to buy us matching speed bikes that we kept at my house. Now it would be my time to come up with a new password.

"So what's it going to be?" Dray asked.

I thought for a minute and then said, "Basketball Jones."

"I like that. What does it mean?"

"Basketball Jones . . . I got a basketball jones for you," I sang.

"So you got love for me . . . huh?"

"Yeah, I got a jones for you, Mr. Drayton Jones. I love you."

"That's what's up, AJ," Dray said, placing a spoonful of fluffy yellow eggs onto my plate.

SEVEN

A couple of days after Dray's homecoming, I walked into Café Du Monde for a cup of my favorite caffeine. It seemed like everybody who lived in New Orleans came here, along with crowds of tourists, so the place was always packed, especially early in the morning when the house specialties, beignets and chicory coffee, were served.

I paid for my coffee and decided it was cool enough outside to sit on one of the benches across the street at Jackson Square. Just as I reached to open the door, someone called out, "Where are you going? I've been looking for you."

I turned around and there at a corner table was Jade, waving and motioning for me to join her. She was dressed nicely in a crisp white shirt and a black pencil skirt, and her hair was pulled back in a ponytail.

"Jade, how are you doing?"

"Doing well. Why don't you cop a squat?"

"Okay, I think I will. I was going to sit in the park," I said as I took a seat.

"Too many crazies over there for me. You know what I'm saying? Where have you been? I've been coming in here every day hoping I'd run into you."

"I had to go out of town. How have you been?" I asked, thinking if she was so psychic, Jade should have known that.

"Did you go someplace exciting?"

"I went to your old stomping grounds, Los Angeles, even though I was staying in Beverly Hills."

"I bet you stayed at the Peninsula."

"How did you know that?" I asked, slightly alarmed.

"It's the best hotel in the city. I used to work there part-time in their spa. And you know I'm psychic."

"It is a nice hotel."

"How is that bitch of a city doing?"

I took a long sip of coffee. "I wasn't there long. How is the job search going?"

"Oh, I got the job as a cocktail waitress, but I didn't get any of the evening shifts yet. I'm making decent tips at least."

"How about that other job?" I teased.

"You mean giving facials and massages?"

"No, the one you came here for." I smiled.

She smiled back. "I haven't met my potential husband. I heard they're not even in New Orleans right now. They're in some place called training camp and won't be here until the end of August. But I can wait," she said with a wink.

"Does Reggie Bush live in New Orleans?"

"I don't know. But I'll find out. I plan to FedEx one of my pictures to him at the Saints office. I know it's not a fresh idea, but it's a start and will get the ball rolling. If that doesn't do the trick, I'll find out the name of the club where the players hang. I might have to go out with one of his teammates first, but trust me when I tell you I will meet him, you know what I'm saying?" she said, raising her cup. "But in the meantime I need to make some money so I can get the right outfit. That way I'm ready to dress like money when that time comes. Real ballers aren't attracted to broke bitches. And I'm not attracted to broke brothas with good dick."

"You strike me as the kind of young lady who gets what she wants," I said, grinning.

Jade smiled back and took a sip of her coffee and then had a surprise question for me.

"So who are you dating?"

"I don't talk about my personal life," I said a little too fast.

"Oh, baby, I heard that. But you're gay,

99

aren't you?"

I didn't mind answering that question. Plus I didn't want any advances from Jade in case she didn't land Reggie, so I nodded and smiled.

"I knew that, and believe me, Aldridge, it doesn't matter to me what box you check. But I appreciate your being so honest with me. You hear what I'm saying? I meet a lot of these down-low brothers and they make me sick with their lying asses."

"I hear you."

"Just tell me what side you butter your toast on so neither of us wastes any time." She leaned in and said, "Don't mean we can't still be friends, right? You never have enough friends, especially when we both new to the city. But you a nice-lookin' man so you probably got a lot of boyfriends or whatever you call them. I had lots of gay friends when I lived in Los Angeles. I used to have coffee with some of them every morning at the Starbucks in West Hollywood."

"I'm very happy," I said. An image of Dray lying in bed popped into my mind.

Jade pulled her cell phone from her purse to check the time and practically jumped up. "I gotta run. I'm meeting somebody about some big money." She finished off the last of her coffee and folded her newspaper, then stuck it in her bag.

Before she put her cell phone in the bag she handed it to me and told me to punch my number in. I did and gave it back.

"Now give me your phone so I can put my number in it. Maybe we can meet for lunch or dinner sometime soon. That way I can keep you posted on my job search and you can make up lies about who you dating and who you not. But I bet you are like me and like jocks."

"You might be psychic, but I know you're crazy, Jade," I said, laughing. I pressed my number into her cell. I was growing fond of her. She was almost the only friend I had in town.

"That's why I like you. It didn't take you long to figure that out." Jade threw me an air kiss and headed out the door.

Later that evening I was in my office looking over sketches for some designs I wanted to show the people at Brad Pitt's organization, when my phone rang. It was Jade. She was crying and asked me if I could meet her at the bar at the Ritz-Carlton, which was one of the hotels that was running full tilt. I'd been to the hotel a couple of times since it was only about three blocks from my house.

When I walked into the bar, I saw Jade

nursing a glass of white wine.

"Jade, is everything okay?" I asked.

"Thanks for coming."

"No problem. Are you okay?"

She gave me a peck on the cheek and said, "I'm okay, AJ. I just needed someone to talk to. I had a date with this guy who stood me up. I guess dudes down here are just like they are in Los Angeles. Plus my landlord is on me for my rent, and not without letting me know that if I give him a little pussy we could work things out."

"Are you serious?" I hoped Jade didn't call me down to borrow some money. I didn't know her well enough to be writing checks for her rent.

"Should I report his ass or just look for another place to stay?"

"You need some money for a deposit if you move," I said. The bartender came over to us and asked me if I wanted something to drink. I ordered a glass of merlot.

Jade continued to tell me how tough it was being single and low on money and how something was going to have to give. She looked so vulnerable at that moment that she reminded me a little of my sister, Bella, only grown up. I told her everything was going to be all right, but wasn't really sure that it would. After all, I hardly knew Jade.

When the bartender brought back my glass of wine my phone buzzed, telling me I had a text. I looked at it and realized it was from Dray. "Who is that girl with you?" I looked up and noticed the restaurant connected to the bar. Dray was facing me with a frown. There was Judi sitting with her back to me, and I wondered if she knew her husband was texting me. I texted him back and told him Jade was just a friend. He texted back, "Make sure you're telling the truth. Also cut your little date short. We just finished our salads and I don't want to chance us coming face to face with you."

I texted back a simple "K" and suggested to Jade that we go around the corner for dessert. I was relieved when she quickly agreed.

EIGHT

By noon Maurice had left three messages, which had me worried. Normally he wasn't the type to chase after anyone. You either got in touch with him or he kept a cool distance until you did. This was something about Mo's personality that I never completely understood. It was as if he kept score, almost waiting for your misstep, which he inevitably would bring up later and throw in your face during the heat of an argument, long after you'd forgotten about the so-called misstep — if you were even aware of it in the first place! I endured the highs and lows of this often labor-intensive friendship simply because after all these years I had an inexplicable fondness for him. Maurice ran hot and cold like a faucet but beneath all the bluster was a basically good guy who suffered from low self-regard. If I had ever had the courage to broach this delicate subject, I'd have told him that his expectations for himself were set so high that no one could live up to them. Instead I listened patiently over and over, while he ranted about one perceived slight or another, the daily injustices that he alone faced, and sooner or later, a quick rundown of my own personal failings as a friend. Fortunately, I understood Maurice well enough to know not to take his jabs too personally — just as important, I knew also how to smooth the situation over before it got out of hand. However, there were times when I asked myself whether our friendship was worth all the extra effort. Weren't buddies supposed to grant one another the space to screw up now and then? Lord knows I cut him massive slack in that department. I guess we take our friends for who they are, all the messes along with the blessings. Maurice talked a good I-don't-care game, but I knew better. There was something sensitive and hopelessly romantic about Maurice.

I remember one miserable rainy evening during the last days of autumn when I got a call from Maurice. From his question "Do you think black gay men will ever learn to treat each other right?" I knew something was wrong. I asked him to repeat his question to make sure I had heard him correctly and he broke down in tears that wouldn't stop. When I showed up at his apartment a short while later, he was still crying.

During the Memorial Day Black Gay Pride festivities in Washington, D.C., Maurice had met Cullen J. Hartwell, one of D.C.'s resident pretty boys, at the big closing party. He was tall and broad shouldered, and a dangerously handsome man with hazel eyes. Cullen was the kind of guy who when he walked into a room — any room — people took notice. It didn't matter if they were gay, straight, or suddenly confused. Maurice had charmed Cullen with his quick wit, but I sensed from the beginning that Maurice thought he was stepping out of his league by pursuing Cullen. He went to D.C. every chance he got, taking rooms in the best hotels since Cullen told him he still lived with his parents and couldn't have overnight visits. Sometimes when I was supposed to pick him up at the airport I would get a call from him telling me he'd decided to stay another night. When I asked Mo how Cullen was in bed, he told me they were waiting until they made a commitment before engaging in sex. Without asking I knew this was Cullen's decision and not Maurice's. He always told me that he had to check out the sex before he would allow himself to become emotionally involved with any man.

In late August, Cullen surprised Maurice

by showing up at his town house, suitcases in tow, and confessing his love for my friend. I had never seen Maurice happier and for the first month I believed Cullen was in love with Maurice. I kept on believing that until one evening when I was invited to the house for a cookout. Maurice was tending to the grill when Cullen made a pass at me. Something I never shared with Mo.

So I wasn't totally surprised when I found Maurice sitting in a dark house at his dining room table, candles flickering, drink in hand, distraught because after spending all day preparing a two-month anniversary dinner Maurice discovered that all Cullen's things were gone. He had been told by another friend that Cullen had moved in with a local television anchorman who was a little better-looking than Maurice and had a fatter checkbook. Making matters worse, it was Maurice who had boasted to the television personality how great Cullen was in bed and how blessed he was.

Cullen didn't leave a loving note or make a phone call about his departure but texted Maurice a few minutes after he discovered he suddenly had more closet space. And though it has been over five years since the incident, I saw something change in Maurice that night, even though he called me the next day with his voice full of laughter, acting as though Cullen Hartwell never existed.

I'd been tied up the better part of the morning in a meeting with Brad Pitt's Make It Right Foundation, presenting some design ideas. The board was excited about my proposals and told me they would get back to me after Brad and his donors had a chance to look them over. Maurice, of course, had no idea where I was and needless to say did not like to be kept waiting. Whatever he had to tell me was urgent enough for him to call three times in two hours, so I phoned him the minute my meeting ended.

He picked up on the second ring. "Where have you been?"

From his jubilant tone, I knew right away that his urgent news had to be good.

"I was visiting this agency I'm thinking about doing some volunteer work for," I replied, more defensively than I'd intended. "I just picked up all your messages at once and was afraid something bad had happened. What's up? Is everything okay?"

The smile in his voice was audible. "Oh, old friend of mine, things couldn't be better. I have some delicious news. Are you sitting down?"

"No, the meeting just ended, and I'm still in their office. Hang on while I step outside."

I waved a quick goodbye to the executive director, as she stood to the rear of the hallway speaking with a colleague who was getting her signature. With Maurice on hold, I passed behind the receptionist seated at his orderly desk in the small but immaculate lobby, where half a dozen would-be tenants waited for appointments, and exited the glass door.

I stopped at the curb, where I laid my portfolio over the top of a public mailbox and removed my sport coat. "Hey, Mo, I'm back," I said, beginning to roll up my sleeves. "So what's the big news that's so important you couldn't wait another second to tell me?"

"Guess."

"Look, with you, I never know. I'll end up standing out here all day in the heat guessing unless you tell me."

He allowed for a dramatic pause, one in which I was no doubt expected to die from curiosity. "Well, since you can't bear the suspense, here goes: I'm going to throw the biggest motherfucking Labor Day party this town has ever seen. All the stops will be pulled out, opulence out the ass, boys for days. In short, I will be the new hostess with the moistest. Atlanta's new grande dame."

"How are you going to do that? Labor Day is less than a week away."

"I know that, boo. I'm talking about next year. A bitch needs time to plan."

So this was the news that couldn't wait. I might have guessed it would be something out of left field. "What happened to Jackson Treat?" I asked, if only to sound invested in his excitement. "He's reigned over the big Labor Day party for years, and I somehow don't see him allowing you to snatch his crown."

I could picture the nasty grin that had to have materialized on his face at the mention of Jackson Treat. Jackson was a tall, ruggedly handsome philanthropist who was widely respected for his work against AIDS in the African American community. That he was also a principal heir to the largest black tabloid in America only set ol' Mo's teeth further on edge. His green-with-envy rivalry with Jackson, who was too much the gentleman to be pulled into a catfight with the likes of Maurice, was a one-sided battle. Although I wasn't in the mood to listen to more dirty gossip, the clownish spectacle Maurice unwittingly made of himself always had enormous entertainment value. This new gambit promised to top everything, and for once I was curious to learn to what new lengths Mo planned to go to unseat his imaginary rival.

In a triumphant voice, he answered, "The wicked witch of Atlanta is about to be dethroned by a much younger, more regal, and far more deserving newcomer than she. Mark my words: that weekend will serve as my official coronation as the new social butterfly of black gay Atlanta." Then he added, none too friendly and with a magisterial sweep of his hand, if I know Mo — "And Mr. Jackson Treat will be banished to wherever aging, balding, thick-around-the-middle black homosexuals with ugly boyfriends young enough to be their children go." At the mention of Jackson's downfall, his voice brightened again. "Now isn't that the best news you've heard in ages?"

Being Maurice's best friend, I thought this would be a good point to step in and try to break the spell he had fallen under. But how do you tell someone as crazy as him that he's lost his mind once and for all in words he might actually hear? The theatrical predictions of his swift ascension — and Jackson's equally swift demise — were comical to say the least. Although I'd attended just a few Labor Day parties over the years, I was well aware that for black gay men and lesbians, that weekend in Atlanta was a bigger holiday than Christmas. For as far back as anyone could remember, the festivities were kicked off Friday night with Jackson's black-tie soiree. His party was followed on Sunday afternoon by the smaller but no less exclusive Lavender Pool Party, hosted by Austin Smith on the estate of his Buckhead home. I simply did not see either man making room for — much less being trumped by — the "new social butterfly of black gay Atlanta." Just wasn't gonna happen, not on their watch.

For starters, Austin too was local black gay royalty. He was a rich entrepreneur who had been featured in the *Atlanta Journal-Constitution*, *Black Enterprise,* and *Ebony,* when they'd done an issue on black millionaire bachelors. The story in *Ebony* had been the source of endless conversation at cocktail parties since Austin was sweeter than a pair of Hostess Twinkies and didn't care who knew about it. Naturally Maurice loathed him for his accomplishments, in fact taking each of Austin's newly publicized feats as a personal affront. That resentment was compounded every year when Austin failed to invite the very obviously social-climbing Mo to his very obviously nouveau-riche party.

Just as I'd expected, Maurice had topped himself — or at least he talked a good game. I was rendered speechless by these absurd ambitions, but I couldn't help ask how he intended to sink not only one diva but two — and on the biggest weekend of the year, no less!

"Oh, don't you worry. I've not yet determined how best to stomp Mr. Jackson Treat, but I can safely say right now that Austin's pool party won't be happening next year — or ever again, if I have my way."

"Mo, what are you up to?"

A public bus thundered past me, advertising on its side the new hit TV series in which Blair Underwood starred as a preacher moonlighting as an amateur sleuth who solved crimes with the help of exotic birds. Jade was an avid fan and couldn't figure out why I refused to watch it. At the moment I had my hands full with the drama unfolding before me.

As if speaking to a child, he said, "Don't you remember that little scandal Mr. Smith got caught up in with the city councilman he was blackmailing for city contracts? I heard the bitch sent most of his money to the Dominican Republic and was building a villa over there. I also heard from a reliable source that he was dating some second-level pro football player who was looking for his ass after talking about their business. I'm told there's a video of them doing the do that's floating around and that Mr. Football wasn't too happy. Now that couldn't happen to a more evil bitch, if you ask me. But you didn't hear that from me."

"No one's asking you," I added quickly, trying not to get caught up in his gossip. Sometimes I had to let Maurice know the black gay social scene in Atlanta wasn't a big deal to me. "But how do you plan to pull off an event so big? A party of that level costs a lot of money. How do you expect to pay for it all?"

"I have my ways. Trust me, AJ. I'll get food and liquor sponsors. Honey, these companies know us sissies have lots of disposable income and they also know how and where we spend it. Paying for the party is going to be the easiest thing in the world. The real challenge will be deciding who not to invite. That list is going to be longer than the list of people who will get the invites! I think I'll call it the 'Glitter and Be Gay Ball.'"

In spite of his harsh remarks and the mean-spiritedness behind them, a small part of me actually sympathized with where Maurice was coming from. I'd never made the A-list either, and there were times when it felt as if these lavish parties were thrown to make ordinary people like Maurice and me feel like shit for not having made the grade. Make no mistake: I wouldn't have participated in those events even if I had been invited. The self-ordained movers and shakers of the black gay social circuit held about as much interest for me as a rodeo. But for someone who's as closely aligned with gay culture as Maurice, the sting of exclusion was clearly felt more sharply. What I couldn't sympathize with or fully grasp was the lengths to which he'd go to right whatever wrongs he may or may not have experienced. When it comes to Mo, it's impossible to know what's for real.

Rather than draw him into an argument about the low nature of this new enterprise, I chose instead to take a less confrontational route in the hope that I might talk a little sense into him. That was the thing you had to remember: Maurice was thin-skinned and quick to anger, but sometimes a well-reasoned talking to — brother to brother — worked wonders.

"I have to tell you," I began in my best therapist manner, "what you're planning is going to take a lot of time. What about your business? You can't neglect your work over this party. Besides, who really cares whether there's a 'fabulous' new party? To tell you the truth, I think there's too much of this stuff going on already in gay life. You can't open a magazine without being hit over the head with the offering of some new gay cruise or huge party. What we need for a change is some substance, something that you don't throw out the next morning when the next fad comes along."

"Child, boo," Maurice said. It was his favorite saying and was the ultimate gay-boy brush off. Like he was telling me, I can't be bothered by the likes of you.

If you could detect a smirk over the phone line, I would have felt it at that instant. "Come on, AJ, when you say things like that I have to ask myself if you're really gay. Do you know how many gay party planners there are in this city? They will be lining up to work this party! I was going to hold it at the penthouse of the Four Seasons but that's in Midtown and so last decade. I think I've finally decided to have it at the Mansion. Won't that be fabulous?"

Clearly what I'd just said hadn't registered. I looked at my watch impatiently, wondering how I might make a graceful exit from this conversation that was spiraling downward. "And why will the Mansion be fabulous?"

"It's only the grandest hotel in Atlanta, and it hasn't even opened yet. My extravaganza will be the first big event held there. Everyone is going to hear about it and wish they'd been there. Oh, I can't tell you how happy I am right now. I knew if I waited long enough revenge would be mine."

A pause hung in the air for a second, as if he were expecting congratulations, with the noise of the lunchtime street traffic instead filling the silence. I wanted to tell him flat-out that this was the craziest, most hare-brained scheme he'd ever cooked up. That it was bound to blow up in his face, and I wanted no part of it. Rather than saying that, I told him, "I guess if it makes you happy, then I'm happy for you." The line went silent again, which I took as my signal to bow out of the call. "Listen, I need to run. I gotta few errands to take care of. Call you later?"

"Why you running off so fast?" he asked, sounding almost hurt. "There's more. The official announcement will be made tomorrow on the TT 2.2 blog. The tongues will be wagging — and I mean that in a good way!" Maurice was talking about Tay Tenpenney, or TT as everyone called him. Tay was the most popular black gay blogger in the country. His blog was called Unsweetened Tea, because Tay wasn't always kind to strangers — or friends for that matter. Nobody dared cross Tay. He not only dropped hot gay and straight gossip like all the other bloggers, but his blog — unlike all the others — was political as well. When people wanted to reach the black gay community, they went to Tay first. Mo knew this better than anyone.

"All of Atlanta will see tomorrow that I have arrived. And I don't just mean gay Atlanta but the whole fucking city, because I'm going to break with tired, old, sorry-assed gay tradition by inviting straight allies to the party too. No point in wasting all that good liquor on a bunch of faggots in black tie."

A young white woman pushing a child in a stroller walked up to the mailbox to post a letter. She smiled as a way of asking me to step aside, which I did with a polite nod. I felt almost relieved to be brought back into the real world by her. Once she'd finished, I returned to my call. "Can't wait to see what you pull together. Let me know if you need a hand."

"You better believe I need your help! I can't do all this by myself. I have something special for you in mind," he said mischievously. "I want you to help me audition the strippers . . . I mean 'waiters' for the party. We'll bring in the hottest boys from across the country for top dollar, then later have them serve me and my good, good girlfriends the 'house specialty' in the VIP area. And I mean the real VIP set. You always have to have a VIP area for A-list guests."

"I'm sure you can handle that all by yourself, Mo." I lifted my portfolio from the mailbox, preparing my exit. "Hey, congratulations. Seriously, I'll call you a little later, okay?"

"You don't sound very excited for me. I thought my best friend would be as happy about my plans as I am."

"I am happy for you, Mo, you know that. It's just that I was in that meeting most of the morning and have some stuff to take care of before the day gets away from me. I want to hear all about it."

"Child, boo," he said with playful sarcasm, "believe it or not, I can take a hint when it's handed to me on a plate, thank you very much. I'll let you go for now, mister, but you'd better call me later. Don't make me chase after you. I can get ugly." Then, as if lost in his own thoughts, he added to himself as much to me, "Like the church queens say, 'God is good all the time.' But don't piss him off."

His question came after the first set of leg lifts and if I hadn't been sitting down I might have fallen over.

"So how long have you known Dray?" Cisco asked.

"Who?"

"Dray Jones, the new point guard for the

Hornets. You must know him. I found out that's who hired me as your trainer."

How had Cisco found that out? Dray went to great lengths to avoid evidence of a connection between the two of us, even going as far as creating a dummy corporation to handle some of the big purchases he made for me. No one in six years had so much as a clue that we were connected.

"Uh, I did some work for him," I answered vaguely, avoiding Cisco's inquisitive eyes. I reached down for a towel to dry my face.

"So are you guys close?"

"What do you mean 'close'?" I started the second set of leg lifts, praying his inquisition would be over soon.

"You know, like bois, or maybe ya'll kinfolks."

"We're not family, but we cool." I tried to sound like someone from the hood, thinking I could pass us off as old college buddies if pushed in a corner.

"You think you could introduce me to him?"

I thought for a second and said offhandedly, "Sure." I was willing to do anything to stop his questions.

"Yeah, maybe he can hook up a brotha with some tickets or a few of those crazy groupie bitches I know he be meeting in

120

every city," Cisco said with a cocky grin.

"Okay, if I talk to him I'll mention it. And by the way, he's not paying you, I am. I just figured a professional basketball player would know the good trainers." Years of covering for Dray made it easy to think fast and lie through my teeth.

But this wasn't over just yet.

"So why did you move to New Orleans?"

Damn! Why was Cisco suddenly so nosy?

"For work," I said, finishing the last set of weights.

Cisco slapped my hand with a high five. "That's what's up. You ready to work your abs?"

"Yeah, let's do that," I said, my body crashing to the mats.

I was looking through a West Elm catalog when my phone buzzed to let me know a new text message had arrived. I looked at the screen and there in all caps was a message from Dray that read, "HEY."

I sent a text back: "Hey." This was his way of letting me know that he was by himself or just thinking about me. It was a small gesture but it always made me feel good. I thought Dray hated living a double life as much as I did, and in some strange way it created a special bond between us over the years. Those texts were especially important when I hadn't seen or heard from Dray for days.

A few seconds later, another message: "What are you doing?"

I wrote back: "Thinking about you."

Seconds later I read: "THAT'S GOOD."

I wrote back: "When will I see you again?"

He responded: "VERY SOON."

I sent back the letter "K" and tried to turn my attention to the catalog, even though furniture was the last thing on my mind now.

Jade stepped in my living room, her heels clicking on the hardwood floors. She paused in the middle of the room and nodded her head approvingly. "I don't know what you do, but you must do it well," Jade said.

A couple of days after our last meeting, she had called to tell me she'd worked her rent situation out and to see if I wanted to go out and get some dinner. I was getting ready to take one of the thick pork chops I'd purchased out of the freezer. I thought it was just as easy to cook for two as it was for one and so I invited her for dinner, which she gladly accepted.

"I do okay," I answered casually. "There are a lot of people in need of my services down here."

"Now what do you do? I forgot." Jade took a seat on my green-and-white-striped sofa.

"Interior design."

She ran her hand through her hair and then twisted her earring with a knowing smile, "I know that pays a pretty penny. Don't you need an assistant or something like the character on what's that show I used to like . . . *Will and Grace?*"

"I liked it too but I've learned from Grace's mistakes never to hire friends. I like you and I want to keep you as a good friend." The truth was I thought Jade might work well for me but Dray wouldn't like the idea of a female assistant. He said they were nosy and talked too much. I told him he was paranoid.

"But if you ever need me, to run a few errands or water your plants, I could do that until you find someone. I can run to the store and go to the post office, and you'd be helping me out because I can sure use the money. I might have to go back to giving facials and massages, because this girl sure isn't going to be trading pussy for rent."

"Does giving facials and massages pay much?" I asked.

"Yes, but some of those rich women got on my damn nerves. Although a few of them can be nice if they think you might come to their house to dust off those pulled-up faces." Jade smiled.

For the first time, I noticed a huge diamond ring on her hand.

"Looks like somebody is doing pretty well," I said, pointing to her finger. The ring didn't look like something a casino waitress wears.

"Oh, this old thing? It's not mine. It belongs to a friend who might be going through a divorce. She doesn't want her husband to know that she charged this on one of his cards before she drops the ball and lets him know that she knows he's been cheating. It's not as big as the diamond Kobe bought his wife. Are they still together?"

"Are who still together?"

"Kobe Bryant and his wife, Vanessa. Because I thought I'd heard they'd broken up. I bet that gold digger got to keep that ring."

"I don't really follow basketball that much," I lied.

"Me either, but everybody knows Kobe."

I looked at my watch and stood up. "I need to go and check on our dinner."

"Something sure smells good. What are you cooking?"

"Pork chops with stuffing and green beans."

"Are you a good cook?"

"I guess you'll know after dinner. You do eat pork, don't you?"

"I eat anything that's free," Jade said from the couch with a hearty laugh.

I went into the kitchen and saw that the food was almost ready. I opened the fridge and saw several unfinished bottles of wine and realized I wasn't being a good host.

I stuck my head into the living room. "Jade, would you like a glass of wine?"

"Do you have any beer?"

"I don't know. I thought you were a wine drinker. But let me check."

I ducked back into kitchen and I heard Jade's voice again. "I changed my mind. Let me have some wine. That's more ladylike."

"White or red?" I called out.

"What's the wine that's pink?"

"White zinfandel," I said.

"Yeah, that's the one. Let me have a glass of that."

I poured Jade a glass of wine and thought maybe I would give her a chance to help me out after all. Taking the glass into the living room, I thought that maybe since we were both new to the city Jade could serve a dual purpose in my life.

NINE

Something was up. I hadn't heard from Dray for over a week and I was starting to worry. Now that we'd gotten past the L.A. incident, our life had returned to normal. I had just finished a run through the Quarter with Cisco, and the workout combined with the humidity had me sweating like I had just come in from a heavy rainstorm. Sitting up on the mat and limp from exhaustion, I could feel his muscular chest pressing against my back as he prepared to stretch me out.

"So that's some good news about your boi?"

"What news?"

Cisco continued to push my back forward. "He and his old lady are having a baby."

I turned around to face Cisco. "What?"

"Yeah, my boi Teddy, who's Dray's cousin, told me his old lady is knocked up. I thought you knew. You two being tight and all," Cisco said, with a hint of innuendo.

My heart was suddenly beating like a bass drum, my mind reeling. I was speechless. Dray had told me they were going to wait at least five years before they even thought about having a baby. That bitch was trying to get her claws deep into him by having a kid. I had always told myself that I would be number one in Dray's heart as long as Judi didn't have a child. I should have seen this coming. I couldn't help asking myself where this left me. If the news was true, it meant Judi had found a way to be in Dray's life permanently. This wasn't the marriage of convenience Dray had led me to believe it was.

"Are you all right, dude?" Cisco asked, clearly confused by my response.

I took a deep breath and said, "I need to take a shower."

"Man, I hope I didn't say the wrong thing. But it looks like all the color has drained out of you, and that's hard to do for black people. You look like you just saw a ghost."

I sprang off the mat and told Cisco to let himself out. I rushed to my bedroom to get my cell phone. I had to talk to Dray.

I closed the door and hit speed dial. The call went straight to Dray's voice mail, so I sent a text saying to call me immediately. I heard the door slam, which meant that Cisco was gone. He must think that I was one strange bird, or maybe he figured out there was more to my relationship with Dray than us just being bois.

The television in my bedroom was on mute but I stared for a moment, lost in thought, at the newly skinny Star Jones talking to the actress Vivica Fox, whose new television show *Court Television* was on the air for the first time. I was happy to see that Star had bounced back. Just as I was getting ready to turn on the volume and hear what they were talking about, the cell phone rang.

"Dray!"

"What's up, boi," he said cheerfully, as if all was right with the world.

"You tell me."

"It's all good. Now tell me who was that young lady I saw you at the Ritz with."

"I told you she just a girl I met in the coffee shop. We were just hanging out."

"You need to be careful who you hang with. Bitches are nosy as hell, boi."

"I know, Dray, and you have nothing to worry about. Now is there something you haven't told me?"

"That I miss you. Yeah, that's true. I really do miss you."

"Then why haven't you called me?"

His tone changed. He had to have guessed there was more to this call.

"Sorry, AJ, but I've been busy. I'm dealing with some issues."

"Dealing with what issues?"

"Some stuff, but nothing that involves you. Just stuff with Judi."

Furious, I paused for a second before blurting out, "Is Judi pregnant?"

Dray didn't respond. He must have been almost as stunned by my question as I was to hear the news from Cisco.

"Did you hear me? Answer me, Dray!" I shouted.

"Where did you hear that?"

"Is it true?"

We sat there in silence, waiting for him to answer. It seemed like forever. I was consumed by feelings of anger and betrayal. How could he hurt me so badly? Finally, in a cold, deliberate voice, Dray said, "I've got to go."

Before I could say "WTF" he had clicked off.

I'd had a couple of martinis and was slumped lazily across my bed in a wifebeater and gray shorts. Dray had hurt me as much as he had angered me. I couldn't think of anything else the entire evening. I was about to switch off the flat-screen television and crawl under the covers when I heard the doorbell ring. I jumped up, figuring it was Dray and he had forgotten his keys. I was suddenly very happy and excited.

I rushed down the stairs and opened the door. Standing in a tight-fitting white T-shirt and a black baseball cap covering a red bandanna was Cisco.

"Cisco? What are you doing here so late?"

"I was in the neighborhood and I saw your lights on, so I decided to see what was up."

Cisco walked into the foyer as if I'd been expecting him.

"What's up?" I asked, puzzled as to why he was here.

"Just chillin'. You looked a little upset this afternoon, so I was just checking to make sure you were all right."

I was touched, yet a little suspicious. So I told Cisco I was doing okay. Something about him dropping in worried me — what if Dray had been with me? But maybe after all, considering where we left off with the phone call, there was little chance of that happening. I decided to be polite and offered him a drink.

"What you got?"

"What do you want?"

"How about some vodka, like some of that

Grey Goose joint."

"I think I can do that. What would you like me to mix it with?"

"Some cranberry juice would be sweet."

I walked over to the bar, suddenly a little embarrassed that I was only wearing shorts and a T-shirt, but, shit, I wasn't expecting a guest. I fixed his drink and made another martini for myself. With him just standing there I realized how lonely I felt and how nice it was to have a man in the house.

"So you just chillin'?"

I handed him his drink. "Actually I was just watching a little television in my bedroom."

"What's on?"

"I don't know, some reality show."

"We can chill up there if it's cool."

"Yeah, that's cool," I said. I started to say maybe we shouldn't, thinking this would be a disaster if Dray did show up, but it would serve him right. The martinis had me feeling a little reckless for once.

I put out my hand in a gesture to let Cisco know he should walk up the stairs first, but in a very masculine move he placed his hand in the small of my back and said, "Naw, you go first." He had an almost sinisterly seductive smile.

I started up the stairs and could feel Cisco

walking closely behind me. Even though I couldn't see his eyes I felt that he was staring at my ass. When we reached the bedroom, Cisco plopped down on the plum-colored chaise longue in the corner.

I turned the channel to ESPN and took a seat on the bed, quietly sipping my drink. The silence was finally broken when Cisco asked whether I minded if he smoked a joint. I didn't like people smoking in my house but said, "Yeah, go ahead." I thought this was funny from a guy who had given me the blues over drinking coffee.

The dim lighting in the bedroom gave a feeling of subdued elegance. All the while I could feel Cisco looking at me, not the television. After an uncomfortable few moments I looked over at Cisco. He took a puff and blew smoke circles between sips of his drink.

With me watching him, he turned his attention to the television. "So you like b-ball?" Cisco asked, without taking his eyes off the screen.

"Yeah."

"Is that how you and ol' boi hooked up?"

"Ol' boi?"

"Your dude who plays for the Hornets. Drayton Jones. The dude who getting ready to have a baby." He blew another smoke circle.

"I told you we just friends."

The mention of Dray reminded me how pissed I was at him and disrupted any guilty thoughts I was having about how it would feel to be seduced by Cisco. I knew that I wasn't going to let that happen, even if he tried. The funny thing about the strange relationship I shared with Dray that was different from a lot of gay couples I knew was that I was completely faithful to Dray. I saw fine dudes all the time, and it wasn't as if they didn't notice me. But I wasn't about to risk the life I had for a roll in the sack with some wannabe thug. Plus I was the old-fashioned type, never one to go around looking for something bigger or better. My mother raised me to be more responsible than that.

Still, I didn't see anything wrong when, after finishing his joint and following it with a strong-smelling blunt, Cisco asked me if I wanted a massage. I was feeling a little tipsy myself and I knew where this could lead, but felt I had the will to stop it before it went too far.

I lay across my bed on my stomach and awaited Cisco's strong hands.

"Take off your shirt. You got anything like some baby oil?"

"I got cocoa butter lotion."

"Where is it?"

"I'll get it," I said, rising from the bed and locating the lotion under the bathroom sink. When I returned my eyes immediately met Cisco's and I looked away.

"Come on, you need to take your shirt off."

I followed his instructions and removed my wifebeater.

I handed the lotion to Cisco, whose intense brown eyes locked on mine. For a long moment I imagined what it might be like to kiss someone other than Dray but put that thought out of my head. I lay down on the bed. My body jolted when Cisco's hands and the warm lotion covered my back. In no time the strength of his hands relaxed my body into stillness.

"You're good at this," I groaned, filling the silence that hovered over the room. I realized Cisco had muted the television. Cisco didn't respond as his caresses sent a sensuous tingle all over my body. A few minutes later, I felt his hands casually pull down my shorts and soon it felt like his lips were teasingly brushing against the small of my back. When he palmed my left cheek with one of his hands I told myself it was time to stop but said nothing.

"So what happened? You took care of ol' boi before he got into the league and now he's taking care of you?"

"What are you talking about?" I asked, focusing on my massage.

"Come on now. I wasn't born yesterday. I think there is sumthin going on between you two."

"We're just old friends from college, like family. That's why I was surprised to hear about the baby from you instead of Dray."

As much as I wanted to stop the massage, I did enjoy him caressing my butt. It was all good until I suddenly felt a huge, lubed finger being stuck up my ass. I quickly turned around and said, "What are you doing?" It was then I noticed that Cisco was stripped down to his boxer briefs and in spite of my alarm I couldn't keep my eyes from moving down his body.

"You know what I'm doing. This is what you want. Right?"

"I thought you were just giving me a massage."

"That's what I'm doing. With a little extra. You know how we do. You take care of me and I'll take care of you."

"I think you should leave," I said as I sat up, looking for my shorts.

"You don't want me to do that. All I'm looking for is an extra couple hundred dollars. That's chump change to a man like you."

"Cisco, you need to leave," I said firmly, but the truth was that I was suddenly afraid of him and worried that he might hurt me.

"What? I'm not good enough for you? I know gay when I'm around it. I see how you be looking at me when we work out."

I slipped on my shorts. "So are you gay?"

"Oh, hell, naw," he said with a dismissive wave of his hand.

"Bi?"

"Nope."

"Then what are you trying to do with me?" It dawned on me that he had come to my house looking for more than company or just a massage.

"Shit! A nigga gotta eat. This could be our little side thing. But you need to know I don't get fucked and I don't suck dick. And I was hoping you could break me off a little paper before I leave."

How did I let this get out of hand so fast?

"Cisco, please put your clothes on and leave," I said, trying to sound as reasonable as possible.

"So, it's like that, huh?" I couldn't tell if he was more angry or hurt.

"It's like that," I said. As much as I wanted him out of my house, I couldn't not look at what seemed to be his big semi-erect dick peering from his white boxers.

"Okay, but I think you're going to be sorry," he said, thrusting a finger at me threateningly. Cisco slipped on his black warm-ups and left without a goodbye.

TEN

After a couple of long, lonely days, Dray bounced into my town house as if everything were cool as a spring breeze. I was not amused. He was wearing a hip-hop outfit of warm-ups, a long white T-shirt, and untied sneakers.

"So what you been doing?" he asked, taking a seat on the edge of the chaise in the living room.

"Waiting to hear from you, asshole," I snapped. It wasn't what I planned to say, but it just came out.

"Come on, Aldridge, don't give me a hard time. You know I have a lot going on. I'm adjusting to a new coaching staff, getting settled in the house, and getting ready for my baby."

I couldn't resist this opening. "I wondered when we were going to get around to that."

"Get around to what?"

"The baby. When were you going to tell

me? Do you know how humiliating and hurtful it was to find out about it from my trainer, or better yet the newspaper and the Net?" Cisco's face flashed in my head and I wondered if I should tell Dray how he had tried to seduce me. I still wasn't sure what all that was about, but maybe that would make Dray jealous and he would realize he could lose me. That's one thing that sometimes annoyed the hell out of me. Dray was so damn cocksure he had me in the palm of his hand, and it might do him some good if he knew I had other options.

"I was going to tell you. But no time seemed like the right time. And I didn't want to tell you over the phone. We see each other so little that when I'm here all I want to do is hold you and make love to you. Besides, do you know how hard it was going to be for me to tell you Judi was pregnant? I already have you feeling sidelined in my life, so I knew hearing about the baby would upset you. There was no easy way to come out and say it."

"You're doing pretty well now, and clearly I'm not the only one you've been making love to." I knew I sounded like some high-school bitch that wasn't getting her way, but I couldn't help myself. I had to know that this was bound to happen. That's what married people did.

"Come on, boi. Married people have babies, and to be honest I'm so happy I don't know what to do. I'm going to be a daddy. Why can't you be happy for me? You feel like I've stuck you in the background and pull you out whenever I like, but without you . . . I don't know how I'd get by. Judi give me things I need sometimes, but what I have with her . . . it's not what we've got. A lot of this stuff is bigger than us. It involves my family, my career . . . shit, you know all this already."

I stood over him for a moment in semi-shock. Here was the man who I had basically given my life to be with gloating over the fact that his wife was about to give him something I never could. The whole world was going to applaud the happy couple while I came up empty-handed. How was I supposed to be happy about that?

It was as if my soul had finally broken, like the New Orleans heat had with the arrival of fall. I should get out of this relationship now while I still had a teaspoon of dignity left.

Dray smiled and took me in his arms. "But don't worry, nothing is going to change between us. We will always be there for each other. You know that."

"Yeah, right. I guess it means I'll just see

less of you. Maybe it's time for me to move on," I said.

"Move on? What do you mean by that? You're not talking about leaving me, 'cause that ain't going to happen, AJ."

"I mean just what I said. Maybe I've been fooling myself. Judi's not gonna stop with just one kid. Before you know it you'll have so many kids you won't know what to do. How long do you expect me to live in the margins of your life?"

"What's wrong with kids? You knew I wanted a big family. My dad wants grand-kids."

"How do I fit into all that?" I asked, exasperated by his denial. I was about to tell him he'd given his parents a home, let one of his other siblings give them grandkids, but I didn't.

"You will always be a part of my life. Aldridge, you know how I feel about you. Don't you?"

"I thought I did," I said softly, sitting down next to him. I wanted him to hold me and say that everything was going to be all right. But somehow I knew it wasn't going to be that way, even if he said so.

Dray moved close to me and put his head on my chest. His head felt as heavy as my heart. I didn't know what to say. I didn't really want to move on, but I didn't want the life I had or where I saw myself heading.

"Trust me, Aldridge, I will make everything work."

"But how?" I pulled away. "Dray, did you hear me?"

"Yes, I heard you. And if you stop asking these questions, I'll leave you these drawers I'm wearing now. I know you'd like that."

"Then . . ." but before I could finish my sentence our lips met and not another word was spoken.

ELEVEN

On a bright September Saturday, I was enjoying a juicy cheeseburger and a beer with Maurice in a midtown Atlanta sidewalk cafe. After my encounter with Dray, I decided I needed to get away and one call to Mo convinced me that Atlanta was the place.

I was looking for support and Maurice was the only really close friend that I had. I often passed up potential friendships because I didn't want to risk bringing new people into my life who might find out about Dray. Cisco proved how easily someone new could blow up in my face.

I'd left the airport and checked into the Intercontinental Hotel in Buckhead, and with nowhere to go and no one to see that first day, I'd done a little shopping at Phipps Plaza. Maurice got back in town the next day after visiting family in Alabama, so this was our first time seeing each other since I arrived.

"I trust the boxes I sent got to New Orleans safely," Maurice said.

"Oh, yeah. I forgot to tell you. Thanks."

"I'm still wondering what exactly made you clear out practically overnight," he said playfully.

"Just needed a change of scenery."

"So do you miss Atlanta?" Maurice asked between bites of the chicken wings he'd ordered.

"Yeah, sometimes. I do miss seeing all the lovely bois in every part of the city."

"You look good, bitch. I think you want to be one of the stars of my party. Are you still working out?" Maurice asked.

"You know me, I'm gay so I got to keep the body tight."

"I'm glad I got almost a year to get my fat ass in shape before the party. Is your trainer any good?"

"Yeah, but I think I might have to find a new trainer."

"Why? You aren't falling in love with him, are you?"

"Actually my trainer kinda came on to me and I turned him down." I took a sip of the ice-cold mug of beer.

"Was he fine?" Maurice asked hopefully.

"He was okay," I lied.

"Then why didn't you give him some of that famous anus?" Maurice laughed.

"Because I'm not like that. I'm a one-man man. You know that."

He pointed his fork at me. "No, child, you're a fool. That's where men are different from females. We aren't built to be faithful. It doesn't matter if you are straight or gay. So if you want to play Goody Two-shoes, give me his digits. I'd sit on that dick and think nothing about it. Do you know how much free dick I'm going to get the closer we get to the party?"

"I'm sure he'd never admit that he came on to me," I said.

"I guess trainers are the new models when it comes to seducing the kids and taking all their coins." Maurice smiled. "A few of them have turned your sister here out. But not anymore. You can get dick just by having power and clout."

"I guess so, because he wanted it to be perfectly clear that he was not gay and not sucking my dick."

"Yeah, right. They all say that. But why didn't you give it a go since you said he was okay? I know that most likely means he was fine as hell."

"Maurice, you know I'm in a relationship."

"You are. Even though I know nothing about this alleged relationship you seem to love hiding from me, your best friend. Have never ever been given the slightest clue as to who he might be or why you're hiding him. But don't mind me. I'm only your best friend. How is that mystery man doing? Maybe I should hold your invitation until you tell me who he is."

"He's fine. As a matter of fact, he's expecting his first baby and I don't know how I feel about that." Maurice was the only person besides Dray I'd confessed this to. I didn't expect him to really get where I was coming from, but it felt good to talk about the situation. "I hope this baby doesn't change things," I said as I watched a group of gay white bois stroll by the restaurant.

"Well, you can't give him a baby unless you're keeping more secrets than I think. I wouldn't worry about it. Those men are usually preoccupied the first three years and then it's back to their old tricks."

"You think so?"

"Child, boo. Just wait until he has to stay home and change dirty diapers."

"I'm sure his child will have a nanny."

"That's right. Your man is rich. Stupid me," Maurice said, playfully hitting himself upside his head. "It's the one thing I do know about him. How could I forget? Maybe I should get a rich man. No, they think they can control everything. Pretty soon I'll have my own money with all the sponsorships I'm getting for the party."

"I thought that money was for charity."

"It is, but there are consulting fees for all my time. Events like this are a lot of work and I need to be compensated," Maurice said.

We ate our meal in silence while the sun beat down on our faces. After a few minutes, Maurice looked at me thoughtfully. "Listen, all kidding aside. Does this guy really make you happy? I mean happy enough to hide a part of your life from your closest friend?"

I thought about his question for a few moments and then said, "Most times."

Maurice shook his head disapprovingly, "When you play with fire, sometimes you get burned, baby."

"He wasn't married when we met."

"So why didn't you leave him when he hooked up with fish?"

"I don't know. Do you ever think of Cullen?"

"Child, boo. Cullen. Please. What do you think?"

Before I could respond, my cell phone rang. I saw that it was Dray calling and I hit the IGNORE button, which would send the call straight to voice mail. A few seconds later he called again and then again. I didn't usually take his calls when other people were around, but I thought this might be urgent.

"Excuse me, Mo, I need to get this. Hello?" I said, standing up. I heard Maurice mumble to himself, "I bet you do."

"Where are you?" Dray yelled.

"What?"

"Damn it, didn't you hear me? Where are you?"

"I'm having lunch with a friend. What's going on?"

"Where? Are you in New Orleans?"

"No. I'm in Atlanta."

"What are you doing in Atlanta?"

"Seeing a friend."

"I need you to come back to New Orleans now, AJ, and I mean right now."

"Why?" Images of my aborted trip to Los Angeles flashed in my head and I became angry all over again.

"Don't ask any questions. I need to see you right away. I need to know who you've been talking to about us."

"What are you talking about?" I walked away from the table and headed toward the entrance of the restaurant. I noticed Maurice's eyes followed me all the way to the door and kept watching from clear across the restaurant.

"Somebody is trying to blackmail me,"

Dray said.

"Blackmail? Are you sure?"

"You heard me. I got a letter in a FedEx package threatening to go to the press and my family about our relationship."

"Did they mention my name?" I asked as I looked over at Maurice, who was now pointing at his watch to let me know he didn't have all day.

"Hell, yeah. They didn't have to say your name. The letter said something about my 'little boi toy' who I moved to New Orleans to be with me. Who have you been talking to?"

"Dray, you know me. I would never do anything to jeopardize your career. Damn it, haven't I proved that to you by now?"

"How else could they find out about us if it's just our secret? You think I told somebody?"

"I don't know," I said, totally flustered. Who could have found out? Cisco threatened that I'd be sorry. Did he have anything to do with this?

"You need to bring your ass back to New Orleans so we can figure this out before I have to respond to this mutherfucker."

"Okay, I'll get the first flight out tomorrow."

"No, today. It's still early. Get on the next

flight tonight."

"But . . ."

"Do it!" Dray yelled, and hung up the phone.

TWELVE

I walked into my house and found Dray pacing like the expectant father that he was, but I knew this didn't have anything to do with no baby.

"What took you so long? It's past midnight. I have to get back home. I need to talk to you," Dray shouted.

"I took the next flight I could get, Dray." I put my bags near the closet door. "Tell me what's going on." I'd given the situation a lot of thought on the flight home and felt more and more frightened for him, than for us. Whatever any blackmailer had in mind was going to hurt Dray far worse than it could ever hurt me. I tried rubbing his arm to reassure him, but it seemed to make him even more agitated.

"Look at this," Dray said, handing me a white piece of paper.

"What's this?"

"Read it."

The words weren't handwritten or typed out, but spelled with letters someone had cut out from magazine and newspapers and pasted to the page.

What will your fans say if they knew you were on the low with AJ?

What would the owners of the New Orleans Hornets say?

What would your father say?

And what would your wifey do?

If you don't want to find out, then I would get ready to reduce your big bank account by one hundred thousand dollars.

Will be in contact soon Mr. DL Basketball Superstar.

My heart dropped to the bottom of my toes. Whoever this was knew way too much and wasn't afraid to use it. But how had they found us out?

"Dray, this can't be real. It's most likely somebody being nosy." As soon as those words were out of my mouth, I didn't believe them any more than I could see Dray did.

"Easy for you to say, but tell me who you told," Dray said, grabbing me. "You sure you didn't tell your little friend Maurice in Atlanta?"

His grip was tight. "Let me go. I didn't tell anyone. I promise," I said.

"What about that girl I saw you with in the restaurant?"

"Jade? I haven't said a word to her."

"Are you sure? You two looked pretty cozy when I saw you."

"Dray, I haven't told Jade anything about us. Now let me the fuck go."

He continued to hold on. "But you said she knew you were gay."

"Yes, she knows I'm gay. I've never mentioned your name to her or anyone."

"Then did you send this? Are you trying to get some more money from me? Is that what this is about?"

Now I was the one ready to get tough. "I'm going to act like you didn't ask me those questions, because I know you know me better than that." I broke loose from him and felt like walking out on his ass right there.

"Then who sent this letter? Someone knows all about me. Somebody is trying to ruin my career." Dray nearly broke down in tears. I'd never seen him like this.

"What do you think the owners of the Hornets will say?"

"Fuck the owners. I'm not worried about them. I'm worried about what my father will say or do. This could kill him. And what about Judi? What about the baby? This could destroy me and everybody I love."

I couldn't keep Cisco a secret any longer. "How well do you know the trainer you hired for me?"

"Who?"

"The trainer. How well do you know him?"

"I don't know him at all. I told you my cousin recommended him." Dray stood up unexpectedly. "Why, do you think it could be him?"

"I don't know, but maybe he has something to do with it."

"Did you say something that could have tipped him off?"

"No, I didn't tell him anything. I was careful as always. But when he told me that you were about to become a dad, well, maybe he read something in my reaction. Hearing the news from anyone but you was like getting hit in the gut with a stack of bricks. I couldn't help but look devastated. There was no way to hide it."

I wondered if I should tell Dray how Cisco had tried to seduce me and how I'd turned him down. But this wasn't the time to get into all that.

"Did he ask you if we were lovers?"

"Not in so many words."

"What does that mean?"

"Could your cousin have told him about the baby?"

"I haven't told him," Dray said.

"Who have you told? Besides, I'm sure it was in the papers."

"I don't know how it got in the papers. These reporters feel like they own me. I told my parents, naturally. That's been it. My wife wants to wait until she's at least four months into the pregnancy. She had a miscarriage before."

"So she's been pregnant with your child before?"

"Yeah, but that's not the point. The only people I've told have been my parents."

"Maybe your mother told somebody. Who is this guy, your cousin?" Dray was always so tight-lipped about his family and I knew he'd be touchy about my insinuating that they might be behind the blackmail.

"Our mothers are sisters."

"Are they close?"

"Sure," he said, massaging his neck.

"Maybe she told her sister and she told your cousin."

"But Butchie wouldn't blackmail me," Dray said, turning and pacing the length of the room. "I give that nigga whatever he asks for. He ain't got any reason to be trying to hit me up for money."

I went over to him and looked him dead in his eyes and asked, "Why?"

"Why what?"

"Why do you give him whatever he asks you for? I thought you said your agent and business manager told your family and childhood friends no when they asked you for money."

"Butchie is my boi and family," he said defensively. "We grew up together. We learned how to play basketball together. Matter of fact he was a much better player than me."

"Then why is he not playing now?" I asked.

"Could never get a good score on the SAT, so he just sort of lost interest."

"Then I think you should double-check with him and ask him more about Cisco. I bet there's a whole lot more going on here, Dray."

"Can't you ask this Cisco dude if he knows anything about it?"

"No, he quit," I lied. "Said something about going back to Atlanta."

"Why didn't you tell me that?"

"I haven't had a chance, Dray," I almost shouted. I tried calming myself before I said something I'd regret. "And it wasn't that important. I was either going to work out by myself or get another trainer."

Dray collapsed into a chair. "I don't know what the fuck to do."

"I think you're overreacting. You've only gotten one letter from this person. Why don't we wait and see if anything else comes?"

"Let someone threaten to go to your father and see how you would feel. I told you about my father. He doesn't understand gay people." I'd remembered Dray telling me about something that happened when he was in seventh grade. His father found out his cousin was gay and forbade Dray to ever spend the night with him. But Dray didn't need to remind me about his dad. I've been his boyfriend for years and he's bent over backward to keep me apart from his family. For a moment I wondered about what would happen if someone exposed Dray and ended this lie once and for all. At least then we could finally live our lives openly and honestly for the first time. But I knew that as closeted as Dray was, even if the truth came out, I was kidding myself by thinking we could live our lives freely.

"Go home and get some sleep and let's see what happens tomorrow," I said.

Dray looked so defeated but picked himself up. "Yeah, you're probably right. Maybe it is a prank," Dray said.

"Now you're talking. Let's wait and see," I said, rubbing his arms again. This time it seemed to calm him down a bit.

He embraced me tightly. "I'm sorry for thinking you had something to do with this, AJ. I know how much you care about me," Dray said.

I hadn't felt this needed by Dray since the news broke about the baby. I was determined not to let him down. I prayed that he wasn't being blackmailed because of something I'd done. I knew this was impossible since I'd never breathed a word to anyone. I had written about our affair in my journals, but I kept those safely hidden in a sealed box.

Dray looked exhausted. "I'll see you tomorrow," he said, and kissed me on my forehead. "I'm under a lot of pressure here but things will be cool soon."

"I know, boi, I know."

THIRTEEN

The moment I saw Jade at Willie Mae's Scotch House, home of the best fried chicken lunch in the state of Louisiana, I could tell something was different. She looked especially vibrant and vivacious and her eyes were twinkling almost mischievously.

"What's going on with you?" I smiled, taking a seat across from her.

"I'm getting close to the prize," Jade said as she rubbed her hands together like she was getting ready for something real good, and I don't mean the fried chicken.

"Close to what?"

"Close to meeting Reggie Bush, and then it's gonna be on! I met one of his teammates at the casino where I work and of course he asked me for a date. I asked him if he knew Reggie and he told me he was one of his best friends. So the way I figure it, I'm bound to meet him."

"Who's his teammate?"

"His name is Steve Slater. He's an offensive lineman, which was clear the moment I saw him. That boi got a big ol' ass and a big head to match. He's cute but not Reggie Bush cute. But I can date him for a minute."

The place was packed, so our waitress hadn't acknowledged us yet. The restaurant had been closed down after Katrina and had only recently reopened. I guess the people in New Orleans missed their chicken.

"Does he know you're after Reggie?"

"Of course not, silly," she said with a smirk. "Do I look dumb to you? This guy Steve is married but his wife is still in Michigan. So there ain't anything I could do with him even if he was my type." Jade looked around impatiently. "What does a girl have to do to get some service around here?"

"How did you find out he's married?" I asked. Dray came to mind all of a sudden. I'd left a message when I woke up, but I hadn't spoken to him today. I wondered if he'd cooled down since yesterday.

"I find out lots of information before I pounce," Jade said. "Besides I'm not going to sleep with him."

"You're not? What if he pressures you?"

"I can handle myself. I'll make it clear I'm not that kind of girl."

A plump girl with a pad, plenty of lip gloss, and a lot of attitude approached us. "My name is Latrelle. May I serve you?"

I set down my menu. "What's the special?"

"Chicken," she deadpanned.

I turned to Jade. "How does gumbo and the two-piece lunch special, dark meat, sound to you?"

"Sounds good to me."

"Anything to drink?"

"Two sweet teas?" Jade said.

"Okay. Salad bar is over there," she said, pointing to the rear of the restaurant. "It comes with your meal."

"I don't want any salad," Jade said, but the waitress had left already.

I couldn't resist asking Jade what she was going to do if Reggie wasn't interested in her.

"Oh, that won't happen." Jade smiled. "You should see me when I fix myself up. It's something to see, honey."

I gave her a little laugh. "Have you ever failed at getting the man you wanted?"

"Just once," she said, holding up her index finger.

"What happened?"

Jade crossed her arms on the table and leaned forward with a sly grin. "Let's just say he fell out the closet when I tried to give him what most guys want all the time. It seemed

161

I didn't have the equipment he needed." Jade laughed to herself.

"Oh, I see." I smiled back.

"What kind of guys do you like?" Jade asked me.

"I don't have a type," I lied.

She sat up and looked me square in the eye, as if she were about to get serious. "C'mon, do you like feminine guys or those homo thugs? What about the down low men?"

"I don't have a type," I said again, and smiled.

"I don't believe that," Jade said with a wave of her hand. "I bet we like the same kind of bois."

"And that would be?"

"Jocks. Right?"

"How you figured that?"

"I told you I'm psychic, silly."

As if on cue, my phone rang. It was Dray. I asked Jade to excuse me for a second and stepped outside the crowded restaurant to take the call.

"Dray, I've been waiting on your call all day. How are you?"

"I got another note," he said, cutting to the chase.

"What?"

"I got a note demanding money and this one had my father's cell number. It said they would be calling him if I didn't meet their demands immediately. I told you this shit was real, AJ."

"Wait a minute. How did they get your father's phone number?"

"I don't know. But it doesn't matter because they have it. I need you to get over and help me figure this out."

"Where are you?" Why didn't this man figure out it had to be somebody in his family? Who else had access to his father's phone number?

"At your place. Where are you?"

"Having lunch with a friend. Do you need me?"

"Yeah, I do, boi. Just hurry up and get here."

"I will."

I clicked off my phone and went back inside. Two sweet teas sat on the table where Jade waited. I told her I had an emergency and was going to take my chicken lunch to go.

"Call me later?" Jade asked with concern in her voice.

I flagged down the waitress as I slipped on my jacket. "I will."

"I got your back, baby," Jade said.

"Thanks, Jade. That means a lot."

FOURTEEN

I arrived home to the sounds of Kanye West blasting throughout the house. I expected to meet Dray in the living room, but his sneakers were the only sign that he was somewhere close by. I followed the music upstairs to the bedroom, where Dray was lying shirtless on the bed.

For a man in crisis, he looked surprisingly calm. He had one leg crossed over the other and his hands behind his head. Dark glasses covered his eyes. When I walked into the room, Dray didn't budge. Maybe he was sleeping.

"Dray, what are you doing? I rushed right back from the restaurant."

"What up, boi?" he replied. Was he drunk or high?

"Can I turn down the music so we can talk?" I said, moving to the CD player.

"If that's what you want to do, but I don't think there's much to talk about." Gone was the panic in his voice from just a while before. Now there was a calmness that was almost more disconcerting than his panic.

"What about the letter with your father's phone number?"

"Kanye's new CD goes hard," Dray said, avoiding my question.

"That's cool, but I didn't rush away from my lunch to come and talk about Mr. West." I was totally confused by his sudden indifference to what only a half hour ago was a crisis.

"You didn't have to leave your lunch."

"You said you needed me."

"I always need you, AJ. You know that."

I sat on the bed and laid my chin on his muscled stomach. "I was worried about you," I whispered. "What happens to you happens to me too. We're in this together, and to be honest I'm scared for the both of us."

He stroked my head. "Don't worry, I'll make sure nothing happens to us." Dray took off the dark glasses to reveal watery, red eyes. He'd obviously been crying.

"So what are you going to do?" I asked.

"I'm going to give them the money," he said matter-of-factly.

"Just like that."

"You heard me. What other choices do I have?"

"How did the note arrive?"

"FedEx. Like the first one."

"Do you have any idea how they got your father's phone number?" I realized suddenly that whoever was behind this had something even I didn't have in Dray's father's cell number. The blackmailer had to be someone in Dray's family or a friend of the family. But how did they find out he's bisexual?

"No idea whatsoever. But it is his number."

"I bet it's someone in your family." Why didn't Dray see that?

"I doubt that," Dray replied quickly, sounding almost insulted. "My family and I are tight. They wouldn't pull some dumb shit like that."

Right. So tight you can't tell them about me, I thought.

"I don't think you should give them the money. I think you should call their bluff."

He sat up. "Why?"

"If you make this easy on them, they may come back for more money or demand something else."

Dray stared at the ceiling, lost in thought.

I sat next to him. "You don't have to play along, Dray. They have no evidence. All we have to do is deny their accusation."

"I thought about that, but I can't let my pops find out." There it was again. Dray's unbreakable devotion to his father and his family.

"Then tell him," I said. "Who knows, he might be cool with it."

Dray looked at me like I'd lost my mind.

"Are you fucking serious? You want me to tell my father that I like dudes? Tell him that I got a boyfriend that I take good care of? Do you know something about my father that I don't know?"

"Like what?" I asked, wondering where this was leading.

"Has hell frozen over? Because that's the only way my pops will accept some shit like this."

"So you got jokes? I'm serious, Dray. Tell the truth. Then we could be together every day and not have to hide. Lead normal lives just like everyone else."

"That is not going to happen. I'm getting ready to have a baby. I'm going to need my father to help me be the best parent that I can be."

"If he's the man you think he is, he will be there for you, Dray. So will I."

"You're talking fantasy bullshit, AJ. This isn't as easy as you make it sound. Do you realize that I got eleven teammates to deal with as well? The NBA ain't ready for some-body to be that truthful. You should hear the shit in the locker room about dudes who came out. I'm not ready to be a spokesperson for nobody but my family and me."

I wanted to say that if Dray's father was as closed minded as he sounded, then he would be the last person to teach Dray how to be a good parent, but I knew despite his father's conservative ways that Dray would always idolize him.

"So what are you saying, Dray? Are you ashamed of me?"

"Aldridge, this isn't about you. This is about protecting my rep. We can't have all this if I'm not playing ball," Dray said as he waved his arms around, gesturing to the town house.

"Well, it's not your rep when it's a lie," I said defensively. Suddenly this was more about our future than the blackmail threat.

"I don't want to talk about this anymore, AJ. I'm going to pay the money. I'm just glad I followed JB's advice and set up a BM account."

"JB? That's your agent, right? And what in the hell is a BM account?"

"Yeah, that's my agent, and he told me I need to have an account set up just in case any unwanted baby's mama shows up and we need to take care of it. I don't think JB had anything like this in mind."

"Promise me you will think about this before you do anything. Maybe we could go to the police quietly and they'll devise some kind of sting."

Dray stood up and turned to face me. "When you gonna get it through your thick skull that this isn't about us? This is about me. My career and future. Don't nobody give a shit if you're gay or straight." Dray's voice was restless with anger.

"So you're saying I'm a nobody? What happens to you has nothing to do with me?" I asked. "Fuck you, Dray." How stupid was I to sit there and try to help this asshole who's telling me that nobody gives a shit about me? I felt like a fool.

Dray grabbed his shirt from the nightstand and put it on in silence. He glanced at me in disgust. As he tucked his shirt into his warmups, he looked around the room for his sneakers and then headed for the stairs.

I couldn't let him leave like this.

"Dray! Come on, dude. Let's talk about this," I said, calling after him.

He had nothing more to say. Instead he stormed out of the house without a word.

FIFTEEN

I needed to get a life.

My own life. Real bad and real quick.

I stepped out of the shower. It had been three days and no word from Dray. Not one phone call, text, or surprise visit, and I was worried that he'd done something stupid. Drying myself off, I wondered if Dray's disappearing like this might help make it easier not to miss him too much if one day I decided to leave him. The thought crossed my mind now and then. But thinking about it was a lot easier than actually doing it.

I spread cocoa butter all over my body, and then slipped into some pima cotton lounging pants with a matching T-shirt. I prepared myself for another day of surfing the Internet and waiting for a man who obviously wasn't coming. Maybe I should go down to the Ninth Ward and see if I could help out there. Make myself useful, as my mother would say.

I logged onto the sports board to see if

there was any news about Dray besides his upcoming bundle of joy or the new contract. Not that I expected to find anything out about Dray being blackmailed, but there was one site called Ballersblog.com that sometimes included gossip about professional athletes. You never knew what would pop up there.

Just as I had pulled the site up, my cell phone rang.

"What's going on, AJ?"

"Hey, Maurice, what's good?"

"Oh, nothing, just looking over some fabrics for some of the outfits I'm going to wear to my party. I plan to change clothes every hour on the hour. Also trying to decide what champagne to serve, and it's going to be hard since all the big companies have sent me free cases. Oh, have you seen Tay's blog today?"

"No, I haven't. What's going on over there?"

"Just a little more mention of the party, which is great because every time I'm on the site I hear from more sponsors. But Tay's going to drop a bombshell that will have the sports world rocking. I think I know what it's going to be."

"What?"

"I can't say because Tay will know it came

from me and I can't have that diva mad at me. Speaking of the diva, he's calling me now. I need to take this, hon. Talk with you later."

"Okay. Keep me posted if you are allowed to share anything," I said. As soon as I hung up with Maurice my phone rang again.

"Hello?"

"Hey, you, is everything okay?" It was Jade. I hadn't talked to her since I left the restaurant in a rush several days before. Although I still didn't know her very well, it was comforting to hear her voice.

"I'm fine," I said in my best attempt to sound that way.

"I thought you were going to call me. You missed some good food."

"Remember, I brought my grub home, and it was great. How are you doing?" I asked, changing the topic as usual.

"I'm doing great. I mean, they working me like a slave at the casino, but I've been meeting some nice people. Hey, do you like basketball players?"

"What do you mean?" I asked.

"Do you like basketball players? You know, is that your type?"

"Why do you ask that?"

"I went out a couple of nights ago with the guy who's going to make sure I meet Reggie

Bush and we were hanging out with some of his boys. After we'd had some drinks they started talking about some guy who plays in the NBA who's gay and who's about to come out. They didn't say who, but I think he might play in New Orleans."

I couldn't believe my ears. This wasn't happening, I told myself.

"Did they say a name?" I asked, trying like hell not to sound as frantic as I felt.

"I don't recall. They said it was a basketball player, or maybe I had too much wine." Jade laughed.

"Are you sure?"

"I can find out," Jade offered, "I'll just ask Steve. I'll tell him I want to make sure my girlfriends don't date him if he's on the low."

"It's probably just idle gossip. Believe it or not, guys talk just as much as girls," I said, trying to act normal.

"Yeah, you're right, but I just thought about you, especially if the guy's somebody nice. Remember me and your love life?"

"Yeah, I forgot. Thanks for thinking about me, Jade," I said, rushing her off the phone. I needed to get off the call quickly. "Hey, can I call you back? There is someone at my door."

"Sure, but don't let me have to track you down again. I don't want to feel like I'm being a pest, but I do worry about you. We all we got in this crazy city."

"I appreciate your concern and I promise to call you, Jade."

"Okay. Have a nice day, sweetie."

"You do the same."

When I clicked off my cell phone, I immediately phoned Dray. It went straight to voice mail.

"Dray, call me ASAP. Please. It's urgent."

"What you need to talk to me about?" Dray stood a few feet behind me.

I threw my arms around him. I was so happy and relieved to see him. "Where have you been?"

"I've been taking care of some business," he said, barely returning my embrace.

All my excitement over seeing him drained right out of me.

"What happened?" I asked.

"Hey, I don't want to talk about it. I'm exhausted. I just came by to chill, not have another argument."

I wanted to say "Hell no" but I could tell from the deep worry in his face and the tightness I felt from his body that he was probably tired from emotional overload. This was one of those times where he needed me to be supportive instead of harassing him about his personal life. I also saw this was not the time to share with him the gossip I'd just heard from Jade.

I reached out to him. "Okay, come over here and let me take your shoes off and we'll take a nap."

"I knew you'd take care of me. Nobody can make me feel better like you, AJ."

"I know, Dray," I said, loving the warmth of his embrace.

"I'm sorry I left like that the other day and had you worried, but I just couldn't take it anymore. To be honest, I was afraid for the both of us. You forgive me?"

"Yeah, of course I forgive you. What's happened over the last couple of weeks would make anyone crazy."

Dray sat down on the love seat in the bedroom. I got on my knees and unlaced his sneakers and took off his shoes and white socks. I rubbed his feet gently for a few minutes, then instructed him to stand up.

I took off his gray "Hornet Basketball" T-shirt and pulled down his black warm-ups. Suddenly, there he stood in just his blue plaid boxer briefs with the hint of an erection.

"Hey, Aldridge," Dray said, sounding to me as vulnerable as a little boy. "I really am sorry. I know you think I'm trippin' and maybe I am, but I couldn't hurt my pops like that. He is everything to me. You never knew your dad, so you might not understand. When I was a little boy, he lost his job and could only find work in Mobile, which was almost six hours away from our home in Mississippi. Seeing him gone all of a sudden, everybody in my neighborhood thought he was like most black men we knew, that he had left his family. But that was not the case. He called us every day and when I had basketball games he made every one of them. My pops told me it was important to him to set an example to me and my siblings so we would become adults he and my mother would be proud of. I'm not saying he's right about everything, but there are certain things I could do that would hurt him, and nothing is so important to me that I would hurt my father. Does that make sense to you?"

"Perfect sense," I responded, touched by his attempt to explain the situation.

"Do you forgive me?"

"Come with me," I said, and dragged him over to the bed. I pulled back the comforter and Dray climbed under the covers. I took off my pants and got in bed with him. I placed my back against him in the spoon position and pulled his arms around me. I felt his face nudge against my neck and I smiled to myself because suddenly everything was right with the world.

About five minutes later, I heard Dray snoring and the weight of his dick against my ass felt hard enough to drill a brick. He missed me. When Dray finished his nap everything would be like it was when he held me so tight. Suddenly I'd be back in a world where everything was magical and perfect.

Sixteen

A couple of weeks passed and everything had gone back to normal. Still, I held my breath the whole time, waiting for the other shoe to drop. But no word from the blackmailer, which I took to mean he'd gotten all he was after.

I woke up late one morning with a dreamy sluggishness and for a moment didn't realize where I was. I knew I wasn't in my own bed, but I felt a body close by. I turned over and there was Dray sleeping beside me. Then I remembered.

He had called me the evening before and told me he wanted to see me, so I did what I always did. I jumped on a plane and checked into the hotel the team was staying at and waited for him to call. We were in Washington, D.C., at the Ritz-Carlton near Georgetown, where the Hornets were preparing to play the Bullets that evening. This was my fifth trip of the season; I'd already joined

Dray in Seattle, Los Angeles, Miami, and Orlando. If the blackmailer had any plans to drive us apart, he was wrong. I loved that Dray wanted to see me more now than he had in months. But maybe there was more to it. He probably wasn't getting a lot of sex at home since his wife was almost six months pregnant. I didn't ask nor did I want to know for sure.

Whenever I joined Dray on the road, I usually got my own room on the club floor and hoped that he would be able to slip away from his teammates before I fell asleep. They didn't have curfews, but he usually hung out with his teammates until they had made their out-of-town booty call connections. Sometimes this lasted till two and three in the morning and it was all I could do to keep my eyes open.

I got out of bed, walked to the large bedroom window that overlooked Georgetown, and opened the curtains. It was going to be a beautiful day. Motionless clouds hung in a perfect blue sky.

"What are you looking at, babe? Come back to bed," Dray said.

"It's beautiful outside. I think I'll go shopping in Georgetown while you guys do your walk-through."

"That sounds like fun. Now come back

to bed."

I kneeled down on the bed and whispered, "Are you hungry? Let's order a big breakfast and put it in the middle of the bed and eat just like we used to," I said, climbing back into bed.

"That sounds like a plan." Dray pulled me close to him and nibbled on my ear. Being in Dray's arms felt like old times and our recent scare felt a million miles away.

"You glad you came?"

"Yeah, Dray. I'm really happy to be here." During times like this, it was like Judi and her bundle of joy didn't exist. This was our world.

"I'm happy you're here too. I always sleep better when you're with me."

"For real."

"Real talk, babe."

"What do you want for breakfast?" I asked.

"Waffles, bacon, eggs, and maybe some cheese grits," Dray said.

"You must be hungry," I teased.

"For food, and something else," Dray said, grabbing my ass.

"I thought we took care of that last night." I smiled.

"Yeah, but I want some more."

"After breakfast."

"Okay, order the food. I'm going to shower

and brush my teeth. The bus leaves for practice a little after ten." He hopped out of bed and ducked into the bathroom.

I heard my phone go off and I saw that I had a text from Maurice asking where I was. He said he'd been calling me with no answer. I sent a text back telling him that I was in Washington, D.C. I started to call him to see if everything was okay, but he texted back telling me to have fun at the Ritz. For a moment I wondered how Mo knew where I was staying, but realized he knew the Ritz-Carlton chain was my favorite.

I looked at the clock and saw that it was five after eight. I wasn't surprised we were off to a late start. Whenever Dray and I were together, we lost all track of time.

I considered the options on the room service menu and phoned in our order. Sitting there, I noticed the elegant room with its cream-colored walls had a stillness that was heightened by the sound of the shower. After all the recent drama, I appreciated the calm.

That quiet was broken when the hotel room phone rang and I picked it up, assuming it was room service checking our order. The Ritz was impeccable and was always checking to make sure everything was just right.

"Hello?" I said.

"Are you enjoying your little visit?" a deep male voice asked in a hard, colorless tone.

"Who is this?"

"Never mind who I am. Just answer my question."

"You have the wrong number."

"I don't have the wrong number. I called the hotel and asked for Aldridge Richardson and they put me right through."

"You have the wrong room," I said firmly.

"This is Aldridge, isn't it?"

"Tell me who *you* are."

"Don't worry about me. Is your basketball boyfriend nearby?"

"I'm hanging up," I threatened.

"That wouldn't be a wise move, playa."

"Why not?"

"Is your boyfriend there with you?"

"I don't have a boyfriend."

"Oh, yes, you do. And if you want to keep him then you're going to get me some big money. Otherwise I'm going to go to the press, wifey, and of course your boi's family. I'm also going to tell your mother what you did when you were fifteen. I don't think she going to like what I have to tell her."

The bathroom door swung open. "Who are you talking to?" I turned around and there stood Dray with a towel around his waist and a toothbrush hanging from his mouth.

"Wrong number," I said, hanging up the phone abruptly, hoping Dray hadn't overheard the rest of the call.

"Did you order breakfast?"

"Yep."

"How long will it take?"

"Twenty minutes," I said, standing up and nervously straightening the room.

"Are you okay?"

"I'm fine," I said without looking at him, "just eager to start the day. I'm going to call downstairs and see if I can get a car service to take me shopping."

"That sounds like a plan," Dray said. He stepped back into the bathroom and pulled the door closed. The phone rang again and I picked it up quickly.

I was in no mood for this. "Hello," I said confrontationally.

"Yes, sir, this is room service. I wanted to ask if you wanted strawberries or blueberries with your waffles?" a female voice asked. "The ticket has both checked by mistake."

"Strawberries," I said.

"Thank you. Your meal is on the way up."

"Thank you."

Just as I hung up, my cell phone rang. I looked down anxiously at the caller ID:

Unknown. I let it go to voice mail, feeling I'd spoken to enough unknown callers for the day.

SEVENTEEN

Sometimes even a twenty-nine-year-old man needs a hug from his mother. But since I was in New Orleans and my mother lived in North Carolina, I settled for the next best thing: a phone call.

I'd been home from D.C. for a couple of days, but I was still upset by the phone call I received at the hotel. I wasn't going to tell my mother what had happened, but I knew she'd make me feel better anyway. I dialed her number.

"I was just thinking about you," Mama said, picking up the phone without a hello.

"I guess we were both thinking the same thing, and how did we ever live without caller ID?" I laughed.

"Ain't that the truth. How are you doing, baby?"

"Okay," I said, halfheartedly.

"Are you sure?"

"Yeah, but why do you ask?"

" 'Cause mamas always want to know that their babies are okay, especially when they're not there in person to see for themselves. When am I going to see you?"

"Very soon. I was thinking about coming up this weekend. First I need to make sure I don't have any appointments with my clients." As always, I hated lying to my mother and wished I could have just said I needed to make sure Dray didn't need me.

"It would be nice to see you, baby." I could hear the smile in her voice. "Bella will be so excited, but I won't tell her until you're sure you can get away."

"I don't want to disappoint her. You think I should call her?" I asked.

"She always loves hearing from her big brother."

"Then I will do that," I said. A beep indicated an incoming call. The ID flashed "Out of Area." Fearing the worst, I took a deep breath.

"Well, let me know when you book your flight. I'll come and pick you up," my mother said.

"I will. Mama, I got another call coming in. I'll phone you in a couple of days. I love you."

"I love you too, baby. We can't wait to see you."

I clicked the phone over and paused to try to calm myself before saying hello. My greeting was followed with dead silence.

"Hello," I repeated, impatience in my voice.

"So I see this is the best number to reach you." It was the same male voice from the hotel suite.

"Who are you calling?"

"You've forgotten my voice already. That's not good, boo."

"Who is this?"

"I told you not to worry about who this is. Just wanted to know when you were going to have my money."

"I don't have any money for you."

"I don't believe that shit. You got plenty of money. Doesn't your basketball boyfriend give you ducats for all that good sex you give him?"

"Stop calling me. I'm reporting this call to the police," I said.

"I wouldn't do that," he warned very slowly. "But if you should contact them, you leave me with no choice but to release into cyberspace the little film you guys made."

"What film?" I asked. Dray and I were sometimes a little wild when we got down, but we never filmed anything. I'd used my digital camera to take a couple of pictures of him in his underwear, but that was it.

"The little film that was made when you were at the Ritz-Carlton. You guys really go at it. Y'all make Kim and Ray J seem like it was their first time."

"I didn't make any film at the Ritz and you know it. Cut this bullshit out."

"I didn't say you did it knowingly. I just said there was one made. If you weren't so quick to get off this phone and if you listen, then you might learn something. The skin-tight black underwear you had on was quite cute and your boyfriend is really blessed down there. I bet you love that."

He was right. I was partial to black underwear because Dray liked the way it looked against my skin. Flipped out by how this asshole would know this, I yelled, "Shut the fuck up. You don't know shit about me."

"Oh, I know a lot about you, faggot. Fuckin' slut! What will your mother think when she finds out about Mr. Wilson?"

"Who is this?" I screamed, finally losing my cool. Nobody and I mean no one knew about Eddie Wilson, especially not my mother. Shit, where was Dray when I needed him? What was this maniac talking about? Had I worn black underwear? I couldn't concentrate. This person had to be bluffing. My mind raced over the faces of people I'd met since I moved to New Orleans and the people I'd come into contact with at the hotel in D.C. There was the friendly bellman who seemed to linger in the suite as he helped me with my bags. The room service attendant and the maintenance man both had been in my room. Did one of them have a hand in this?

"Think of it this way: I'm your filmmaker and if I don't get paid, then I'm going to have to release this little gem."

Now it was my turn to bluff. "You don't have a film of me."

"Wanna bet? This little film is going to have more hits than the R. Kelly and Paris Hilton sex tapes combined. With it being a big-time basketball star and his boyfriend, everybody going to be downloading that shit. Don't you love this cybershit? Maybe I'll have that old-school jam 'Basketball Jones' playing in the background as you two get busy."

"Yeah, right," I scoffed. "You don't have shit." But he'd said it: *basketball jones.* Did this asshole know about my and Dray's secret password? How could he?

"You don't believe me? Give me your e-mail address and I'll send you a few frames of your first feature film."

"You got hold of my phone number. If

you're so clever, try getting my e-mail address too."

"That won't be a problem. I think after you review your performance with your boyfriend, you'll change your tune."

"Fuck off," I said, and switched off the phone in a huff.

A wave of anxiety washed over me. I wanted to call Dray, but I didn't. I hadn't yet mentioned the hotel phone call to him because he'd been so excited after he'd hit thirty-three points, which included six three-point shots in a row. I always got a text after the Hornets won, but after that game I not only got a text but a phone call as well. Dray was so excited, happier than I'd heard him in weeks, that I didn't want to bring him down with more bad news. Truthfully, I thought maybe I could take care of this on my own. I just prayed this entire situation would go away.

This phone call meant that either somebody was playing a sick practical joke or that Dray and I were in really big trouble.

EIGHTEEN

I flew to Atlanta for the day for a haircut and to get my teeth cleaned, since I hadn't found a good barber or dentist in New Orleans yet. Dray was busy worrying about his pregnant wife, so I figured he wouldn't even notice if I was gone for a day. Frankly, I was relieved to get away for some time of my own. I secretly hoped that when I returned all would be right with the world again.

My intentions were to fly down in the morning and come back on an evening flight, but instead I called Maurice for an early dinner and he convinced me to come to his house for dinner and then spend the night. Since I didn't have any plans, I gladly accepted.

After eating some delicious down-home Southern food takeout from Justin's, Maurice and I retired to his den to catch up over a couple of bottles of wine. Dray had been so much on my mind that I'd forgotten to take care of myself. Maurice had been there for me over the years, and I missed these times and our talks more than I realized.

Maurice poured his fourth glass of white wine, chattering away about his party, which he no longer referred to as simply "the party." In a nod toward grandeur — real or imagined — he had given it the illustrious-sounding name "Glitter and Be Gay Ball." Whatever he called it, there was much about the whole setup that still puzzled me. Apart from how Mo planned to pay for everything, even with sponsors, there remained the unanswered question of how he and TT had become so tight. Everyone knew that TT was the gossip to end all gossips and that there was no depth so low that he would not dig for dirt. But what I'd heard also was that behind TT's flashy-trashy persona was a big, snobbish old queen who thought he was royalty; in other words, exactly the kind of "uppity bitch" Mo railed against. Although I enjoy a word of gossip now and then, as a rule I steer clear of this type of gay man. People like him made me grateful to be with Dray, no matter the obstacles and occasional pain involved. Maurice, however, was not altogether outside this world. In fact, I sometimes thought the only thing that separated him from the likes of TT was that he didn't have his fame or money. But it was more than this that distinguished them. Mo didn't run in TT's celebrity circles, and breaking into that group was about as easy as crashing a party by scaling a barbed-wire fence wearing a tuxedo; you could give it your best, but chances were you'd end up getting shredded.

I was mulling all this over my wine when it occurred to me that this might be the perfect moment to do a little digging myself. Up till now he'd purposely kept the details of his sudden connection to TT ambiguous, which for him was like waving a red flag. Maurice had been going at the bottle pretty good, and his tongue by now had to be at its most loose.

Trying my best to sound nonchalant, I asked offhandedly, "Hey, Mo, tell me again how you and TT got so tight? Where did you meet him?"

A smile of superiority flashed across Mo's face, indicating he was about to share a story that he quite obviously enjoyed but wasn't entirely sure he should tell. As much as he enjoyed this story, however, he enjoyed his wine even more. I therefore knew it wasn't a question of whether he would spill the beans but how many he would spill. Given his current state, I wagered it would be the whole pot.

"Like everybody these days, we met on-line. But not on one of those gay dating sites," he hastened to add, as if that were something beneath him. "I simply wrote TT an adoring e-mail, saying how much I admired him for what he'd accomplished, how I followed his blog religiously and worshipped at his shrine. He wrote back almost immediately, we exchanged a few friendly notes — including one with a picture attached of me looking particularly stunning — and then just like that he invited me to lunch. The Capital Grille, of course. It was all so simple that I couldn't believe he fell for it."

"What do you mean? Fell for what?"

"You know me, child," he said with a playful slap on my knee. "You have to get up pretty early in the morning to trick a diva like me, but do I ever know how to work these star fuckers. All I had to do was oh-so-casually drop the names of one or two people who knew."

"Knew what?"

He grinned once more, then looked me in the eye as if to heighten the moment of suspense. Then he added bluntly, "About his sordid little life in Miami before he moved to Atlanta and became the black gay grande dame. How he got the money to finance his rise to the queen of the gay gossip blogs."

Leave it to Mo. Yes, he could be low-down and devious, but at times like these, I have to admit, he had me in his corner, fascinated by what new mess he had concocted. I smiled to myself in anticipation, while Maurice finished off his wine glass and poured himself another. I knew that wine was like a truth serum and since I had been drinking, my so-called moral code disappeared along with the wine.

"Tay grew up down in Miami, right outside of Little Havana, and was a hustler coming out of the womb. When he graduated from high school, he moved to South Beach, where he was dating this thugged-out nigga who also happened to be one of the city's biggest drug dealers. The dude had bank and nobody ever knew he was on the low, but they had been messing around for a long time. Well, old boi used to like to slap Tay around like he was a real bitch after he'd had too much Henny, and I guess one day Tay got tired of being smacked like he was a rag doll. And so like any diva, Tay started plotting his revenge."

"How the hell did you find that out?"

Settling back into the black leather sofa, Maurice paused. Whether this was for dramatic effect or he actually was attempting to gather his thoughts, I couldn't say. I'd seen him toasted before, but he wasn't quite there yet. That was only a matter of time. More than likely this was part of his performance, and knowing Mo, he relished it. Here I was, his captive audience.

"You see, a couple of years ago I met this guy through a site that posted profiles of prisoners looking for pen pals. You have to pay to get their addresses and stuff but the company that runs the site stands by all the profiles and pictures as being legit — not like most of these sites, where everybody is serving up fake pictures. Anyway, I was intrigued, so I wrote to about ten guys — all the same letter, naturally — and eight responded. Most of their letters were barely legible, but they were hot! Men in prison ain't got no shame while they in the joint."

I'd been listening so intently that I'd almost forgotten I was holding a glass of wine, so I took a sip. "But what does this have to do with Tay? Was he in prison?"

"No, honey. We both know Tay wouldn't last a night in prison. No, it was his boyfriend Dillard Lewis, better known as 'Big Dil,' who was in prison. I know because he was one of the inmates I wrote to. He had a body to die for and I'm telling you, I'd have held out waiting for him over the two years

196

he claimed he still had left to serve. Well, you know these guys. They'll tell you anything to keep you on the line. Wasn't any two years — more like forever. But I didn't know that when we first met."

Maurice then leaned in toward me without a word, the way they do in movies when someone is about to deliver the goods. I followed suit and leaned toward him expectantly. Our heads inches apart, he said, "And can I tell you this man wrote me some letters that made me wetter than morning dew! I'm telling you," he squealed, throwing back his head at the memory, "I used to get hard just walking to the mailbox. Where he came up with this shit, I'll never know, but I was falling for this nigga — and just through his letters! That nigga made your sister wet with his words, baby."

He let out a little laugh, perhaps embarrassed to have revealed himself to me so suddenly, but that wasn't Mo's style; more likely he was turned on all over again just talking about those crazy letters. He then took a white cocktail napkin from the table and dabbed his glistening brow. I couldn't help but wonder how Mo had held out telling me this story — one he obviously prized — for so long.

"Things progressed from there," he continued. "Soon I was put on his phone list, and suddenly I was getting calls from him at least twice a week. Phone calls from prison are expensive but worth every penny when they talk nasty. And if that man could write dirty, Lord, you shoulda heard him talk dirty! AJ, as God is my witness I was done! I mean, sold on this motherfucker. People joke about this prison-love shit all the time but, I swear, when it happens to you, it's a whole other story." Maurice was the only person I knew who for emphasis could turn "whole" into a six-syllable word. "Asking no questions, you pick up and go meet your man. So the next thing I know, I'm heading down to some skanky prison in Florida I'd never heard of to meet my new husband. You'd have loved it. I drove the entire way with the top down, feeling just like Whitney Houston in *Waiting to Exhale.* I was going to meet my man."

Now it was my turn to laugh. I shook my head in disbelief. "I'm speechless, Mo. I mean it. I'm outdone. You gotta tell me what happened when you met."

"Well, for starters, he was even better-looking in person than in his pictures. I would have sold my grandmother back into slavery to touch him but of course they didn't allow that shit in prison. It's fine for those guards to stand by while some dude gets gang-raped, but when it comes to two grown men giving each other a hug, forget it! But believe me, I went back every chance I got. What can I tell you? I was obsessed, maybe even possessed. I couldn't get enough of the man. If you saw his picture, you'd know just what I mean."

"Where does TT come into all this?"

"I'm getting to that, be patient. Let the diva have his moment. One day I told Big Dil about me moving into a new apartment in Atlanta, and he said rather ominously that when he got out he was coming to Atlanta to settle a score. When I asked what he meant, that's when I found out about him and Tay."

"What about them?" I asked, surprising myself by how invested I'd become in the details.

Maurice simply sat there for a moment, swirling the wine in his glass. "It seems old Tay is a very smart diva indeed. He wanted out of the relationship, but there wasn't any way Big Dil was going to let him go just like that. Remember, he used to knock him around but good. Tay must have gotten desperate because he cooked himself up a nice little plan. There came a weekend when he knew Big Dil would be driving up to Orlando to see one of his baby mamas. Totally on the sly and without Big Dil having so much as a clue, Tay packed a suitcase full of drugs, guns, cash, you name it, then stuck the suitcase in the trunk of Big Dil's car. Next Tay tipped off the authorities, who stopped Big Dil on the turnpike, and Mr. Big Dil hasn't seen the stars in the sky ever since. Tay set him up big-time."

From the zeal with which he spoke, Maurice obviously bought the story, but it rang hollow to me. I didn't doubt that a relationship that fucked up got out of hand and crazy games were played out, but it all sounded far-fetched, even for a drug-dealing thug and his boi.

I chose not to put any of this into words and instead went along with Mo. "Wow! That's an incredible story. It's almost hard to believe. This really happened?"

"Please believe, child. I thought it was kind of crazy at first but it all makes sense when you think about it. Doing so much illegal dealing, Big Dil didn't trust in banks, so he kept his money at home, and eventually Tay got his hands on it. It doesn't take a genius to guess that someone at Big Dil's level of dealing thought nothin' of leaving millions of dollars lying around. But who'd have figured Tay had the balls or know-how to pull off the job? Big Dil didn't know it then, but he sure as hell knows it now!"

"That's a big job all right." I set my glass down on the table, intent to get to the bottom of this, if there even was one. "But what was that about him telling you he was getting out in two years?"

"Yeah, that's what he told me when he had me under his spell, but it didn't take long for me to figure out he was lying. That nigga is gonna be in jail for a long time."

"For how long, do you think?"

"Right now he got life or something, which means I ain't never gonna get any of that dick. He told me he has close to twelve inches and thick."

"That's what I'm talking about." With the mention of Big Dil's off-limits foot-long, Mo's story somehow felt much sadder to me. But I wasn't going to get sidetracked on dick gossip. "So he's sure Tay set him up?"

"No doubt about it, and get this: that crafty bitch took all the money that he didn't put in that suitcase and moved to Atlanta, where he completely remade himself and started his now thriving business. When he found out over lunch that I knew Big Dil, he was ready to deal. To put it plainly, I need him to bring down Austin, which is no skin off Tay's nose. What choice do I have? Nobody would give a shit if the information about Austin came from me. Who'd listen?

Despite what this sounds like, it's not black-mail. Even I got to draw the line somewhere. I don't want any of Tay's money, just a little bit of his power. He scratches my back and I rub his."

"That's some story," I said, wondering how much of what he'd spilled would be remembered in the morning.

"Yeah, it's one motherfucking story all right," he concluded with self-satisfaction. Then Maurice sat straight up. He looked serious all of a sudden, as if he'd realized he'd talked too much. "But it's our story, AJ, and if you tell anybody — I mean anybody — both our asses will wind up living in Idaho in witness protection. You can't breathe a word of this to anyone. Do you hear me?"

"You ain't got to tell me but once," I said. "Besides, I'm pretty good at keeping secrets. Even better than you know."

Maurice nodded his head in appreciation, raising his glass in a toast. Whether this was in recognition of our friendship, the party, his dealings with TT, or all three, I'll never know.

"Why do I have to change my plans?" I asked.

"Because I really need you to be in Chicago with me, babe. You bring me good luck," Dray said, taking my hand.

"But I promised my mother. I won't cancel on her twice."

"The Chicago game is big. It's for first place and you've been my good luck charm lately. I've been scoring thirty points or more every game and it's because you're in the stands. I'm convinced of that. Besides, I get to hold you all night."

Dray had come by after his morning practice and we were having blueberry smoothies in the living room. I had decided to tell him about the new threats but when I saw how geeked up he was from practice, I must have lost my nerve. Instead of telling him about the phone calls, I said I was going to North Carolina for the weekend.

"I'm not the reason you're doing so well. You've been playing well all season. You're a great basketball player, Dray."

"Come on now, baby boi. Chicago is a wonderful city and I might see if I can stay a day extra, since we don't have a game until three days later. Maybe we can find a spa outside the city and do something special." He smiled.

"You guys play Chicago later next year. What if I come then? I really need to get home."

"I don't know," Dray said. His face softened with disappointment. He took my hands and rubbed them together as he thought it over. Finally he let out a sigh, then turned to meet my eyes. His face broke out in a grin. Dray moved in real close and traced my lips with his tongue. I'd longed to taste his tongue all morning, but I decided to let him kiss me first.

"Those are kind of tasty," Dray purred.

"My tongue tastes better," I whispered.

"I bet it does." Suddenly his strong tongue entered my mouth forcefully and we locked in an embrace.

We kissed passionately on the couch until the phone went off in the next room and shattered the moment.

"I need to get that," I said, pulling away.

"No, come back here. You can't leave me like that. I want more," Dray pleaded.

"Only if you say I can go to North Carolina this weekend. If you do that I promise to join you in Toronto for the next game." Dray knew that was my least favorite NBA city because it was so cold, although it was the one place where he didn't mind venturing out with me for window-shopping.

"Okay, you win. But if I have a bad game in Chicago, it's going to be your fault," Dray warned.

The phone stopped ringing but immediately resumed seconds later.

"Let me take this. It might be a bill collector." I laughed.

"Yeah, right. You don't have any bill collectors. I make sure of that. But you go ahead. I'll be upstairs taking a shower. I expect you to join me in a few minutes."

"Okay, I'll do that," I said, giving Dray a quick peck on the cheek. I hopped off the sofa and sprinted toward the hallway where the phone was located.

"Now hurry up," Dray said as he walked up the stairs.

"Sooner than you think. You just make sure you're ready." I waited a beat, then clicked on the phone. "Hello?"

"I see your boyfriend is there to offer a little afternoon delight. How special is that?"

I was not about to do battle with this guy while Dray waited, so I simply clicked off the phone and headed toward a stress-reducing shower upstairs.

NINETEEN

I walked through the automatic doors of the Raleigh-Durham airport and into the cold North Carolina night. The fresh air against my skin reminded me how chilly Raleigh got this time of the year. But just being back home warmed me with nostalgia. I crossed the sidewalk, passing several cabs, when I spotted my mother waving and blowing the horn of her ruby-red Cadillac. Her smile immediately made me glad that I had passed on Chicago.

"My baby's home!" Mama sang as she got out of the car and hugged and kissed me.

"Hey, Mama. So good to see you and be back home."

"And we're so glad you're back home."

"Where is Bella?"

"Having pizza with one of her friends from dance class."

"A female friend I hope."

"You know my rules, Aldridge," Mama

said, cocking her head. "Bella doesn't date or take phone calls from the opposite sex until she's sixteen, and then only if her grades are right." She slipped her arms over my shoulders. "Come on and put your luggage in the trunk. We need to move fast because I'm parked illegally and I don't want to argue with the rent-a-cops."

Mama popped the trunk and I laid my garment and overnight bags over her tennis rackets and Bella's worn ballet slippers. I couldn't help but notice a bag of golf clubs and thought how wonderful it was that my mother had taken up the game in her fifties. It pleased me that Mama finally had her own life apart from Bella and me.

"You want me to drive?" I asked.

"You might not remember how to get around this town. Raleigh is really growing," she said, turning over the ignition. "Before long it might be too big for Bella and me."

"I bet I can still find my way around this town."

"You can certainly borrow my car if you decide to go visit some of your friends."

I thought for a moment and realized that no one I wanted to see lived there anymore. Like me, most of my classmates had left Raleigh, for Atlanta, Washington, D.C., or Charlotte. Besides, the people I'd been close to during my senior year at East Side High weren't my classmates or from Raleigh. I suddenly remembered Devin Gossett, the track and field star from Shaw University. I'd met him coming from my summer job at Bank of America before my senior year in high school. Devin was my first serious romance and I couldn't help smiling at the memory of sneaking out of the house and into his dorm room after I was certain Mama had fallen asleep. At the time she was working two jobs, so I could usually count on her being out cold by 8:30. Sometimes I would ride my bike to the campus or Devin would borrow one of his teammate's cars and meet me blocks away from Mama's house.

The last time I'd heard from Devin was several years ago, when he had gone back home to the Bahamas to compete in the Olympics for the national track team. He told me then that he was marrying a girl from the islands, not because he was in love, but because it was what his parents and country expected of him. Little did I know this would become the story of my life. That was cool with me because I liked Devin a lot but never felt in love with him like I did with Dray.

Meanwhile Mama was talking about her

golf game, the new outlet malls, and how she wanted to come down to New Orleans and help Katrina victims. Every now and then I would look over and catch a glimpse of her brown eyes, which were soft and full of a mother's love. She was wearing a rose-red sweater, with an ivory skirt and lipstick that matched her top. Mama was a petite woman, short, just a little over five feet, with no visible waist. As a kid, I thought she was the most beautiful woman ever. She's still striking all these years later.

About twenty-five minutes later, we pulled off Highway 85 South and drove down a few dark roads until we came to the gate of a charming neighborhood. On both sides of the street stood two-story homes with spacious yards dotted with leafless trees. I remember the look of wonderment on my mother's face the first time she saw her new house fully decorated by yours truly. It was a look that I would never forget, and it had brought me great joy to be able to purchase a new house for my mother and sister. Thanks to Dray's generosity, I'd been able to pay cash for the house and decorate it with stylish furniture that had always been out of Mama's reach. He knew how much family meant and told me to pull out all the stops if it was going to make Mama happy. I loved

Dray even more for allowing me to make that happen.

Mama's place was a white two-story house with a long brick walk leading to the door. We pulled into the driveway and into the garage; I got my bags from the trunk and followed Mama through the garage door and into the kitchen. The sudden aroma of the kitchen was almost as welcoming as my mother's hug and kisses, but not quite.

"What's that I smell?" I asked, laying my bags on one of the chairs in the breakfast nook.

"You know I had to cook some of your favorites." Mama went over to the stove and took a big wooden spoon from the counter and stirred a simmering pot.

"You left food cooking? Now you know better than that. You could have burned this house down," I scolded.

Hands on her hip, she gave me a "Who do you think you're talking to?" expression. "I knew that your flight was on time, so I left it on very low. I wanted it to be hot when we got home."

I joined her at the stove, "I thought we'd have pizza like Bella, but is that what I think it is?"

"What do you think it is? Or better yet, what does it smell like?" Mama asked as she lifted a silver lid from the big steel pot.

"Is it your world-famous stew?"

"You got it, baby. I know what my number-one son likes."

Mama was known for her white bean stew with duck sausage. My favorite dish was seasoned with chopped onions, minced garlic, fresh thyme, and miniature tomatoes. She usually served the stew with a warm spinach and bacon salad along with garlic cheese bread on the side. I could tell from the fragrant aroma that this had to be the exact menu. Mama knew me so well. I had even been thinking about the stew as the plane took off.

"Bella's gonna hate that she missed this." I laughed.

"That girl doesn't know what good food is. I told her she wasn't assured my good genes and she needed to start eating healthy if she wanted any kind of serious dance career."

"She'll be all right. I think we both know she got good genes."

"Sit down, son. Let me fix you a bowl," Mama said.

"You want me to help? I can get the salad plates." I looked around the kitchen, trying to remember which cabinet Mama kept them in.

She waved a dishcloth at me dismissively.

"Sit down. You know my rules. You're a guest on the first night, but first thing tomorrow I'll go back to treating you like family."

"Do you have any red wine?" I asked.

"I do, but don't let me have to tell you to sit down again. I will get it when I finish serving the food."

I sat down at the table and unfolded the white linen napkin and placed it in my lap. I watched my mother ladle the stew into a white bowl, and somehow the joy she felt in having me home came through even in the small gesture of fixing my plate. All of my problems back in New Orleans felt a lifetime away.

There really was *no place like home.*

A couple of hours later, I was in my bedroom on the computer, trying to see if the Hornets had won and whether Dray had had a good game. The Hornets Web site said that they had lost the game and Dray had scored twelve points — not bad, but certainly not the scoring tear he'd been on recently. I wondered if he was going to be upset with me. I picked up my phone and sent him a text message. "Keep your head up boi. Y'all will get them the next time. Sleep well. AJ."

I then sent Jade a text reminding her to check my mail and water my plants. She texted me back immediately telling me it was already done.

I then got a text from Dray: "See I told you so. Next time you should listen to me boi."

I texted him back a simple "K" and then got up and walked over to my suitcase, which was lying open on the bed, when suddenly the door opened. A delightful, fine squeal of a teenage girl exploded in my room.

"My big brother's home! My big brother's home!" Bella repeated as she raced toward me, nearly tackling me onto the bed.

"Bella, you look so pretty," I said, kissing the top of her head. She had on a light pink leotard, a blue hoodie, and pink sweatpants that I'd sent her months ago. Her hair was in a ponytail and her skin so smooth and silky that if I hadn't known better, I would have sworn she was wearing makeup.

"AJ, how long are you going to be here? Maybe you can come to my dance studio or we can go shopping at Belk's. Did Mommy tell you that I'm taking voice lessons and that we're going to get an interview coach or maybe a life coach?"

"A life coach? An interview coach? What's that? Sweetheart, when did you get a life?" I joked.

Bella eyed me sternly. "I will be a junior in

high school next year. And the interview coach helps me with my pageants, taking me through mock interviews."

"Are you ready for that?"

"Ready? My book bag is packed. I can't wait to go to a new school and leave some of those petty middle-school girls behind."

"So how is that going?"

Bella picked up one of my magazines and let out a sigh. "They just hatin'. I guess it's to be expected. If Paris and Nicole can endure it, then I guess I can as well." Bella sounded quite the grown-up. I regretted that so much of my time was spent away from her and Mama. Here she was becoming a young woman and I was missing out on all of it.

"Paris and Nicole? Are they in your class?"

"No, silly. Paris Hilton and Nicole Richie from *The Simple Life.* I love those girls."

"I don't know if those are good role models, Bella," I said skeptically.

"I know they do stupid stuff like drink and drive, but they're going to stop doing that. I wrote Paris on her Web site and she actually sent me a letter back." Bella was clearly impressed by the connection she'd made. I didn't want to tell Bella that most likely Paris's assistant or some secretary had penned the response.

So I said simply, "That's nice."

"How long are you going to be home? I wish you would move back here so you could see me dance all the time."

"Maybe someday we'll live in the same city. The three of us."

"Mommy said we were going to watch a movie tonight. Which one?"

"I brought *Dreamgirls.* Have you seen it?"

"Have I seen it? Please," she said, looking at me sideways. "Only ten times and I know all the songs and dance steps. I tell my dance teacher all the time that I'm going to be the next Beyoncé." Bella dropped back onto the bed and waved her skinny arms.

"Why don't you just be the first Bella?" I suggested.

"Yeah, that's what I'll be. Everyone will just call me Miss Bella." She giggled, staring at the ceiling. "And I'll make so much money that I'll be able to take care of you and Mommy like you take care of us."

I closed the suitcase and sat it on the floor. "Well, Miss Bella, why don't we go in the kitchen and microwave some popcorn and get something to drink."

She popped off the bed. "Okay, and I'll even make some of my famous Bella's pink lemonade."

"What am I gonna do with you?" I teased, slapping her butt playfully.

Bella stretched her arms out playfully and sang, "And you, you . . . you. You're gonna love me. Yes you are. Ooh . . . love me."

"Hey, I thought you wanted to be Beyoncé not Jennifer Hudson," I said, pulling my little sister out of the bedroom and toward the kitchen to prepare our snacks for movie night.

TWENTY

I had been home in New Orleans for a little over thirty minutes when the phone rang. I looked at the caller ID, recognized Jade's cell number, and clicked on. "Hey, Jade."

"So you made it back safely," she said. "Did you enjoy your trip? How are your mother and little sister?"

"They are doing fine and it was a really good trip. I'm glad I went home."

"Glad to hear it. What's your little sister doing? Did you tell her about how you're planning a sweet-sixteen party for her?"

"She's into school and her dance. I didn't mention the party because I want it to be a surprise." I settled on the couch. "What have you been up to?"

"I've been keeping myself busy. I picked up some night shifts and even work the VIP room at the casino. They've been calling me a little bit more at some of the spas to do facials, so I guess the rich people must be moving back to New Orleans. I have to go to some woman's house in a little while. I guess the bitch too rich to leave her house." Jade laughed.

"It's good to hear the rich people are returning. Maybe the city is on its way back at last. Anything important looking come in the mail?" I asked.

"Nothing looked urgent. I checked your e-mail too and I printed everything out and set it on the table in the hallway."

I looked at the narrow table right off the living room and noticed a lovely assortment of colorful flowers. "Hey, thank you for the bouquet. It's nice to come home to fresh flowers."

"I thought you'd like them."

"I do. I may have to leave town more often if it means flowers will be waiting."

"Listen, I need to start getting ready for my appointment. Do you need me to bring your key by today?"

"It can wait. Thanks for looking out, Jade. Don't forget to send me your invoice."

"I won't forget that!"

"Maybe we can get together soon and grab a bite to eat," I suggested.

"That would be nice. Maybe I'll try to learn how to cook something." Jade laughed.

"If you expect to marry a football player,

you might want to work on that," I teased.

"You're probably right."

"Is that all you want from life, Jade?" I asked, suddenly thinking about Bella and myself.

"What do you mean?"

"Do you think marrying a ball player will make your life wonderful?"

There was silence for a moment and then Jade said, "I got big dreams, AJ. I want to own an exclusive dress shop, carrying dresses I design myself. I'm pretty good at it. But most important, I want to be happy and in love. Now if that happens to be with a street sweeper, that's who I'll marry."

"For real?"

"AJ, you haven't figured it out. I'm a lot of talk, but I'm really a good girl."

"I know that, Jade."

I heard the beep indicating I had another call. "Oh, Jade, make sure you marry a man who brings you flowers," I said.

"I always wanted to live in a house where flowers were waiting on me, so you don't have to worry about that."

"I'm glad to hear it. Bye, sweetheart," I said, and clicked over to the other line.

"Hello?"

"So, I see you're home." It was the black-mailer back to haunt my ass. Anger welled up inside me and I wanted to throw the phone against the wall.

"What do you want?"

"We'll get to that later. Have you checked your e-mail?"

"No."

"I think you should do that and then we'll talk about how you're going to give up all that money that doesn't belong to you."

I'd listened enough and clicked off in a fury. I walked straight to my home office. My hands were shaking from a combination of nerves and anger as I punched the power button on the computer. It took a minute for the computer to boot up and then I logged on. The silence was broken by the automated voice saying, "You've got mail."

Several new messages had arrived that morning, but one e-mail captured my attention immediately. The sender's name was BLACKMALE and the e-mail came with an attachment. The message read, "Thought you might like to see this before the rest of the world does. Mr. Wilson would be so proud of you."

I couldn't begin to imagine what I was about to find, and part of me wished I could shut my eyes and make the whole thing disappear.

When I opened the attachment, a pop-up

appeared at the bottom of the screen.

I clicked on the PLAY button, which started a film clip showing two men in bed. I looked closely. Even though I couldn't see the faces clearly, I realized that it was me and Dray at the hotel in Washington, D.C. There was no audio and the screen was so tiny that the movement was hard to make out. But it was clear to me that it was us, just as it would be to anyone else who knew what we looked like.

Dray and I were passionately kissing and undressing each other, something we did often when we had the chance to be alone. Someone had invaded the most intimate, cherished space of our private life and I felt sick to my stomach. I quickly shut down the e-mail and rushed to the bathroom. Standing in front of the toilet, I didn't know whether I was going to cry or throw up.

I looked into the mirror and couldn't help but notice the look of fear in my eyes. I had tried to keep it cool and thought I could handle the blackmailer all by myself. Suddenly I saw how wrong I had been. But I didn't need to see my reflection to know I was scared. I turned the cold water on and splashed my face repeatedly, trying to calm myself with deep breaths.

I dried my face and headed toward my

bedroom to do something I hadn't planned. I was going to tell Dray it was quite possible that he was about to join the elite club of celebrities who had a sex video on the Internet.

"Dray, please call me when you get this message. I need to talk with you right away. I know you have a home game tonight. Maybe you can stop by. It's urgent." As soon as I hung up, my landline rang. I knew exactly who it was.

"So what did you think of my little film?"

"What do you want?" I asked in a surprisingly calm voice, even though my pulse was beating so fast I could feel it in my neck.

"I'll tell you what I want. I want you to get me a quarter of a million dollars — don't breathe a word of this to anyone — and then I want you to get your faggot ass out of New Orleans," he said with mounting anger.

Had I done something to this guy to offend him personally? My mind ran through all the people who might have a score to settle with me, but I came up blank. But maybe it wasn't me but Dray they were mad at, and I was caught in the middle. Was Dray holding out on me? Did he have somebody else in his life besides Judi and me? "How soon am I supposed to do this?" I asked, not knowing what he meant by getting out of New Orleans. This was so far out of control now that I wondered if it was time for Dray and me to go to the police. This situation didn't appear to be about the money, and what assurances did I have that this guy still wouldn't release the video even if I followed his orders?

"Just stay by the phone," he warned. "I want the money in cash and I'm warning you, if you tell anybody or show up with someone you and your boyfriend are going to be the talk of cyberworld. Do I make myself clear?"

"Yes," I said.

"I guess you're smarter than I thought," he said smugly.

"How do I know this still won't end up over the Internet after I've paid you?"

"Guess you'll have to trust me."

"So when I give you the money you will get me the original copy of the video?"

"That's the deal."

I knew full well that even if he gave me the original it was no way of preventing him from double-crossing me. This idiot was right about one thing, I was going to have to trust him.

"When do I get the video?"

"As soon as I get the money and I know your ass is out of town for good."

"Why do I have to leave town?" This part of his demand was worse than extorting money from me. While I didn't much care for New Orleans, I cared for Dray deeply, and if Dray moved to Timbuktu I'd have followed. This man wasn't intent on just taking our money: he was hell-bent on tearing us apart and destroying our lives.

"Because that's the way sh . . . because I said so. Stop asking so many damn questions," he said.

The practical details involved in moving so quickly came to mind. "I might not be able to sell my house very quickly," I said, wondering why I was talking real estate to this total stranger.

"It's not your house. Your faggot boyfriend bought it. Remember?"

I'd had enough of this guy and my patience ran out. "Look, let's get this over with. Where do you want to meet?"

"Jackson Square," he said, just as my cell phone started ringing. It was Dray, and a protective calm settled over me even though I should have been more scared than ever. Maybe together we could beat this guy.

"I'll wait on your call, but I will need some time to get the money."

"You better not be trying to stall. All you got to do is go to the bank."

"I got to go," I said.

"Expect my call soon," he said, and hung up.

I immediately clicked on Dray's call.

"Dray. You got my message?"

"Hey, baby boi. No, I haven't listened to my messages yet. I just left the locker room on my way home but I thought about you and so I just called. What was your message?"

"Not so good," I said, wondering if I should tell Dray over the phone.

"What happened?"

"I don't think I should go into it over the phone."

"Okay. Hey, guess what? I felt my baby kick today. I went with Judi to her doctor's visit and I felt him kick. He'll be here before you know it." Dray sounded like he was beaming.

"It's a boy?" I asked, trying not to sound as deflated as I felt.

"Yeah, that's the other good news. I'm going to have a boy."

I sank back into my sofa speechless, my mind reeling that not only was Dray going to be a father, but this woman was going to deliver a boy. Just what Dray had hoped for. What else could go wrong today? I asked myself as I stared at the back of the front

225

door. I felt so alone all of a sudden. I wanted to walk out that door and out of this whole sordid mess and into a life where I was the star, or at the very least costar.

"Aldridge? Hey, are you still there?" Dray asked.

A few more moments and I finally said, "Yeah, I'm still here."

"Isn't that great news? My parents are so proud. My dad is already talking about teaching him how to play basketball like he did with me."

"Yeah, Dray, that's wonderful news," I said, forcing myself to sound as supportive as I could. "Can you come by tonight?"

"Naw, dude, I promised her that I was coming home right after the game. I'm going to have to play ghost for the next couple of months because she's going to need me a lot more. But don't worry, I'll make it up to you soon, or maybe you can come to Phoenix next week when we play the Suns. Do you want to do that?"

"If you want me to," I said halfheartedly. Sure, she needed him. I wanted to pour out all my news about the blackmailer and say, "See, I need you too, Dray." But just as I done a thousand times before since he met Judi, I held it in.

"Hey, I'm pulling into my garage. I will

text you before I go to bed."

"Yeah," I said, feeling tiny tears begin to slide down my face. "Why don't you do that, Dray?"

TWENTY-ONE

After several martinis all by myself I lay down to sleep, but instead only dozed on and off. Was I really about to lose everything? I could stand losing the house and I could even stand losing all Dray's money if it came to that. But the thought of not having Dray in my life was something I couldn't fathom. I needed him and I hoped Dray needed me too.

I woke up and found there was a text from Dray saying he was going to try to sneak off and come see me. So when I heard the doorbell a short time later, I figured he'd run off without his key.

"What the hell are you doing here?" I demanded.

"I wanted to see how you were doing. We didn't leave on such good terms," Cisco said.

I couldn't believe that this asshole, who had to be behind the blackmail of Dray and me, had the nerve to show up at my home. Maybe he didn't think I would be home and was coming to my house to plant some kind of movie camera or listening device to further his plan.

"Aren't you going to ask me in?" Cisco wore a Puma sweat suit that was a kelly green color with yellow stripes I hadn't seen a lot of men wearing. Funny that in the heat of anger I noticed something as dumb as that.

"Why would I want to do that?"

The expression on his face suddenly changed from all smiles to a deep frown. "So it's like that," he said, taking a step back and looking me up and down like I wasn't shit.

"Yeah, that's the way it is." If I could have popped him upside his head, I would have.

He looked visibly alarmed.

"So, are you still working out?"

"Are you kidding me? I can't believe you'd have the nerve to show your face. Did you come to pick up your money? Is that what you're here for? You guys aren't giving me much time. I ought to call the fucking police right now."

"Police? What are you talking about, dude? You don't owe me any money."

"Come on and stop playing with me. I know you're the one who blackmailed Dray,

and now you're doing the same thing to me."
I eyed my alarm system to the left of the
door and made sure I knew where the panic
button was in case this fool came after me.

"Blackmail? Dude, you trippin'. I'm here
to apologize, but if a brotha can't drop by to
admit that he was wrong, then I will just take
my happy ass home."

I scrutinized Cisco to see if he was possibly
telling the truth. He had to be behind this
scheme, and most likely one of his bois was
helping him out. I didn't know how they
were getting their information but I figured
their street smarts could carry them only so
far. But if he really was behind all this, why
would he come to my house? The terms had
been laid out by the blackmailer, so why
would he risk exposing himself by seeing me
in person?

"So," I said, my arms crossed against my
chest, "you're saying you didn't contact
Dray and threaten to tell his father if he
didn't give you $100,000 and then turn
around and put your bois up to do the same
thing to me? You didn't threaten to release
some little video of us if I didn't comply?
Are you saying that wasn't you?"

Cisco stepped closer, as if to plead his case.
"Look, man, that ain't the way I roll. I make
my own money. I might not ever have bank

like you and Dray, but my moms raised me better than that."

Don't ask me why, but somehow I knew there was not a trace of a scam about him. Maybe he was telling the truth, and here I was acting like a crazy person.

I followed my hunch. "You sure?"

"Look, Aldridge, my word is my bond. I don't know what you're talking about. I came over here to apologize for coming on so strong a few weeks ago. I was wrong and that was unprofessional." Cisco stood there a moment, looking expectantly, as if my believing him was the most important thing in the world to him.

Frankly, I didn't know who or what to believe anymore. My nerves were fried and I didn't have the strength left to fight this alone. I had to talk to someone.

"Come in," I said, opening the screen door.

He backed away hesitantly, playfully, putting both hands in front of himself defensively. "Are you sure?"

"Yeah, I'm sure." I laughed. "Things have just been crazy lately. Come in."

Cisco slid into my living room like a stray cat who might get tossed out at any second.

"So will you accept my apology? I think you're a cool dude and I can help you find a good trainer. I just wanted you to know that you didn't do anything wrong and I'm working on some issues in my own life."

"No hard feelings," I said, shaking his hand. "You owe me an apology? If anything I owe you one."

We took seats facing each other across the coffee table.

"So what's all this about being blackmailed? That's some serious shit."

Now that I'd gone and told him about the blackmailer, there was no turning back. I couldn't exactly turn around and say this was some type of joke I'd planned just to pass time. I had to play it cool enough not to tell him too much, but just let him know what I was up against. "Yeah, that's the real deal. At first they came after Dray, and when he paid them a hundred thousand they came after me."

I went on to tell Cisco about the guy demanding money and meeting him at Jackson Square.

"I wouldn't be meeting any niggas in any park in New Orleans carrying a suitcase full of money. Dude, this sounds like some television or movie shit. And you thought it was me? That's funny," he said, shaking his head, amused by the idea. "I ain't got the smarts or the heart for that kinda shit. My ass don't want to end up having the state of Louisiana providing my housing."

With Cisco out of my lineup of suspects, the field was suddenly wide open. Only it made less sense than ever.

"Who could be behind all this?" I said, thinking out loud.

"Sounds like some shit these junior playas in New Orleans might try. Punk asses." Cisco leaned forward. "Do you need my help? I got my bois that could put a little pressure on these people," he said, slamming his left fist in his open right hand as a show of power.

"What can you do? What are you saying?"

"I'm saying I got some associates who can bring the wood and ain't nobody got to know."

"Let me think about it." As much as I loved the idea of the blackmailer getting his ass kicked, I didn't want to get involved in anything criminal that was going to get my ass into trouble that Dray's money couldn't get me out of.

"Okay, man, but all you got to do is to say the word. I will hit up my boys and it will be on like *Donkey Kong.* Shit, I ain't busted up a pimp in a long time."

I laughed in spite of myself. "I'll let you know, Cisco."

"Okay, that's what's up. I'm going to bounce, but hit me up if you need me. My cell number is still the same."

"I appreciate that," I said.

"That's what's up," Cisco said, and leaned over and gave me a brother-man hug. I walked him to the door.

"Thanks for coming by. I really appreciate your concern."

"No doubt," Cisco said with a smile that belied his tough-boy demeanor.

An afternoon rain was beating down on the roof of my town house when Dray walked in, soaking wet.

"You miss me, baby boi?" he asked, seemingly unaware of the irony that he was about to have a new "baby boi" all his own. He removed his T-shirt, his six-pack glistening.

"Yeah, I missed you."

"How you gonna show me you missed me?" Dray asked. He was oblivious to all the new drama, and that would have been almost funny if I hadn't felt so afraid and alone.

"You want a massage?"

"That could be a start."

"I'll do whatever you need, Dray. You know that." I knew where this was heading and I started to tell him what I really wanted was to just crawl in bed with him, maybe read to him until we both fell asleep. I needed him to hold me like old times when we were in college, to tell me that everything would be fine just as long as I was in his arms.

Dray unbuckled his belt and his jeans slid down. In seconds he was butt-ass naked. His dick looked as big as a telescope.

"Come here, babe, and show me how much you missed me," Dray said devilishly. I needed to talk to Dray more than I needed to make love to him, but his awesome body was dictating the conversation. After all these years, this man made me hard as brick any time we were together.

I walked over to him and he wrapped me in his massive arms. He began kissing me and his kisses were so deep it was like he was making love to me with his lips. I was ready to climax right there in his arms.

"Let's go into the bedroom," I suggested, removing my sweat suit.

"Naw, let's do it in here," Dray whispered in my ear, which he proceeded to nibble like some exotic delicacy. He was feeling frisky and I needed to be made to feel safe. I gave in to his passion. Before I did, however, I picked up the remote to my music system. I clicked it and the melodious sounds of Keyshia Cole filled the room.

Dray was sprawled out with an expectant smile. I crawled over to him and started to lick him like he was covered in chocolate syrup. As I got to his groin, I could smell the heavy scent of his arousal. He cupped the back of my head to pull me in closer, moaning, "Come here, AJ baby, and let Dray show you how I really feel about my boi."

Dray's massive dick was fully erect, begging to be stroked and tasted. I slid my hand over his mushroom head and down his long shaft all the way to his balls. He closed his eyes, lost in pleasure, moaning, "Oh, baby, that's it." I repeated the gesture, running my tongue over his dick head at the same time. Finally I couldn't stand it any longer and took him in my mouth in one quick motion. Dray shuddered and opened his eyes. He mouthed a silent "O." I closed my lips tight around his dick and then went all the way down on him, coming up only to kiss his balls.

When it felt like Dray couldn't stand it anymore, he stood up and went to the French Provincial desk where I kept my condoms and pulled a couple of the gold packets out. Then he came over to me from behind and began to grind on me as he played with my dick until it was brick. He turned me around to face him and he bent down and began kissing my chest until I was ready to explode from excitement. He began kissing me deeply and then he turned me back around. Moments later, I suddenly felt his latex-clad dick plunging into me like someone was pushing a balloon up my ass. I gasped, half in pain, half in disbelief that this man could slide inside me so fast. I offered no resistance, pushing my ass into him, wanting every inch in me. As he began to grind, the pleasure intensified and I didn't want him to ever stop as he sent a sweet excitement through my body.

I closed my eyes and enjoyed the cool slipperiness of the lubricant before letting out a long breath of pure pleasure. I could feel Dray's warm breath against my neck and the faint smell of his deodorant as he continued with his powerful strokes. As he pumped harder I reached back to touch his plump, muscular ass like I was trying to press him deeper inside me. As the ripples of pleasure streaked through my body, Dray and I were moaning as our sweaty passion increased.

"What you want me to do now, baby?" he whispered.

"Oh, Dray, keep fucking me. Come on, boi!"

"You like that big dick, boi?" He began to stroke me deeper and faster, mounting me doggy-style.

"I love it," I said, trying to hold up my nut.

"Like you love me?"

"Yes . . . yes," I said. I lost myself completely at the sensation of having Dray inside me.

"Tell me."

"I love you, Dray." I could barely get out the words, he had me so breathless.

"What else you love?"

"You."

"What else, AJ?"

"I love this dick," I moaned.

"How much?"

"I can't live without it . . . oh baby, that is it!" Dray's muscled body enveloped mine, squeezing tightly. In a moaning and pumping crescendo, we suddenly climaxed simultaneously.

As we both lay on the polished cherry floor, limp from exhaustion, there were so many unspoken questions dancing in front of me. I looked over and admired Dray's eyes and lips, and his dick lying on his belly like a turkey drumstick. I wanted to kiss him but I resisted. Dray looked at me and asked if I felt all right and I simply nodded my head. I wanted to ask Dray if Judi made him feel as good as I did. Did she love him the way I did? Could he be himself when he was with her? Could he tell her every thought that crossed his mind? I wanted Dray to promise me that we would always be together. That he would always love me. But nary had a word left my lips. Although we lay there wrapped in an embrace, I could feel my man slipping away between my fingers.

TWENTY-TWO

The big day arrived and I was nervous as hell. How exactly do you walk into your neighborhood Bank of America and withdraw a quarter million dollars in cash? Although I told myself that I was going to do it no matter what — after all, what choice did I really have?

Still, somewhere in the back of my mind I resisted. Maybe this wasn't the answer. Dray had paid off this guy before — what was to stop him from coming back again? I still hadn't told Dray a thing and kept asking myself if that wasn't a mistake.

It wasn't as if he knew how to handle the blackmailer all that well. He had caved in at the demand, anything to save his ass. But even so, we had been in that together and for some reason that had made a difference, made the situation feel a lot less scary than it felt this time around.

I told myself that I kept Dray out of it because I loved him with all my heart or I was scared of what he might do. Whatever the reason, I was going through with my plan without a word to Dray.

I walked into the bank loaded with identification and an empty Louis Vuitton duffel bag. I decided to make my transaction at mid-morning, when I thought it would be less crowded. The last thing I needed was someone nosy overhearing my business. There were enough people spying on me as it was.

There were only three people in front of me and they couldn't move fast enough. When my time came, a young African American woman with two-toned hair asked how she could help me.

As calmly as I could, I said, "I would like to withdraw two hundred and fifty thousand dollars from my SmartMoney account, and I would like it all in hundred-dollar bills." No matter how I tried to psyche myself up for that moment, I couldn't quite get it right. I'm sure I looked as suspicious as I sounded. I had more than enough money in my account, but I was still nervous about taking out such a big withdrawal and walking around with it.

"You want to do what?" she asked with one

of those "sister-girl-child, please" looks.

Just as calmly, but no less nervous inside, I repeated, "I would like to withdraw a quarter of a million dollars from one of my accounts and I would like it in hundred-dollar bills."

"I guess you want crisp, new hundred-dollar bills," she wisecracked.

"That would be nice, Nikita," I said, looking down at her name tag.

"I'll need some identification."

"I have three pieces," I said, handing her my Louisiana and old Georgia driver's licenses and my black American Express card. For good measure I had my dog-eared social security card on stand-by.

She looked at my identification, then at me, and then once again at the cards.

"Where did you open your account?"

"In Atlanta," I said.

"Is that where your signature card is?"

"I guess so."

"What's the last four numbers of your social?"

"Eight-one-one-nine," I said, from memory.

She clicked my information into the computer in front of her. "What is your verbal password?" she asked.

"Basketball thirteen."

"Hmmpt. There it is," she said, sounding surprised. She sized me up, as if to figure out where I got all this money and what I was going to do with it after I made the withdrawal.

I gave Nikita a quick smile, hoping to speed the transaction along.

"I have to talk to my supervisor, and this may take a minute."

"Take your time, Nikita," I said. "I'm not in a hurry."

About ten minutes later, Nikita came back, smiling, with a middle-aged white female. I could see a middle-aged black security man out of the corner of my eye. Nikita sat back down at her computer and proceeded to explain my transaction in detail. Then the supervisor looked at me and asked politely, but sounding concerned, "Mr. Richardson, is everything okay?"

"Everything will be just fine once I complete my transaction," I said firmly.

"I understand. We're waiting for your Atlanta branch to fax us a copy of your signature card since you're not a regular customer at our branch. I expect it any moment." She smiled again, eyeing me more than a little suspiciously.

"And how long will that take?" I asked.

"Not long. But I hope you understand,

we're trying to protect you," she said. I started to say, "Yeah, by keeping me from my own money," but I didn't see any advantage in playing my angry-black-man card, so I simply smiled back politely. Nikita still looked at me with a hint of suspicion, like she was thinking, What is this nigger up to?

"Why don't you sit in my office while we get this finished for you," said the supervisor, who identified herself as Mrs. Curtis.

"That sounds like a great plan," I said as I looked to the glass office off the lobby that she pointed to.

"I'll join you in a few minutes," Mrs. Curtis said.

"Fine. I'll be waiting," I said, heading toward the office.

Inside the office I noticed a couple of certificates on the wall. I learned that Debbie was her first name and that she had an undergrad degree from the University of Alabama and a masters from Southern University. I'd heard that there were a lot of white people in the area who'd gone to the graduate and professional schools of the predominantly African American Southern University. Somehow I couldn't picture Debbie Curtis being one of them. Just as I was getting ready to look closer to see what kind of degree Debbie received from Southern, she walked in, carrying a blue bag and noticeably friendlier. She closed her door quickly and took a seat behind her desk.

"Thank you for your patience. I was able to verify everything and complete your transaction, Mr. Richardson," she said as she began to remove hundred-dollar bills from the bag. "This sort of transaction, in such large amounts of cash, is highly unusual for us. I hope you understand." She laid out the stacks of bills in front of me. Once the surface of her desk had nearly been covered with money, she said, "I would advise you to count it, although I can confirm with absolute certainty it's all there."

After ten minutes of counting under Mrs. Curtis's watchful eye, I nodded to her as if to say, "That's everything." I opened the duffel bag and began to place the bills inside. She had gotten clearance but her demeanor told me she couldn't figure out what the hell I was up to.

"Would you like me to get one of our security officers to walk you to your car?" she offered. "That's a very large amount of money."

"Thanks, but that won't be necessary." I had my own security in the form of Cisco waiting on me right outside the bank. He had offered to be my bodyguard when I handed over the money in the park. Although I figured this asshole wasn't about to try to hurt me, having Cisco close by did offer some comfort.

"Well, thank you for banking with Bank of America, Mr. Richardson. Maybe sometime soon you can come in and sit down with someone from our brokerage. We might help you to invest some of your remaining funds. We'd be happy to speak with you anytime," Mrs. Curtis said, offering me her slender hands.

"I'll think about that, but I have someone handling my investments for me right now. Thanks for your help with this matter."

I headed out of the bank with Nikita's eyes following me, a smirk on her face.

When I got back home, I waited for the phone call with further instructions. Clearing out wasn't going to be easy. I looked around the house and thought I would miss this place. I recalled the first time Dray saw the place decorated. He walked in and his mouth dropped open. He said that I'd outdone myself and maybe one day we'd share a place like this.

Dray and I had had some good times here and I really believed I could be a lot of help in rebuilding the city. But somebody else didn't think so and wanted me gone, baby, gone.

Right at noon my landline rang.

I took a deep breath. "Hello?"

"Did you get the money?"

"Yes, I did," I said.

"Good. Now I want you to meet me right in front of the fountain on the square at five thirty sharp. Don't be late and the money better all be there."

Ignoring his threat I asked, "When will I get the disc?" I wondered why he wanted to meet in a place so public. There would be dozens of witnesses. Could he be afraid of me?

"I told you when you'd get the damn disc."

"Oh shit," I said, suddenly remembering that I had a seven o'clock flight to Phoenix to meet Dray for his game.

"What's wrong?"

"Can we meet a little earlier? I have something I have to do early this evening."

"Hell no, and make sure you don't tell anybody or you'll really be sorry."

"No one knows," I lied. Cisco made me promise I wouldn't attempt the drop-off alone.

"If anything seems funny to me the whole deal is off and that won't be good for you."

"How will I know you?"

"I'll be dressed in black," he replied quickly.

"What am I supposed to do when I get there?"

"I want you to sit on the bench on the west side of the fountain with the bag with the money right next to you. Just look straight ahead the whole time. You'll know it's me when I arrive. I will take your little package, make sure everything is straight, and then I'll give you what you want. You do what I tell you and this won't take long."

"Okay," I said, looking at my watch. I wondered how I was going to explain missing my flight to Dray. Where would I begin? "Sorry I missed my flight. I had to meet my blackmailer." I needed Dray more than ever.

"Be smart and all your troubles will be over."

"Five thirty?" I said.

"Five thirty sharp."

I clicked off and suddenly I found myself wondering what you wore to a blackmail drop-off.

When I arrived at the square, I saw no one dressed in black. Instead there was a group of young guys throwing a football and the usual smattering of tourists strolling through the park. I saw in the distance — across from the square — Café Du Monde and thought of Jade. She'd been the one reliable, good friend I'd made in town. I felt lousy about ducking out without telling her. Until that moment I'd not realized how much I'd miss Jade.

As instructed, I took a seat on a bench on the west end of the fountain. It was well past 5:30 but no one had shown. Just as I was wondering if this was some kind of joke, a black man, about five-ten and close to two hundred pounds, walked toward me wearing all black. This fool had a tarnished gold-colored grill in the front of his mouth. The first thing that came to mind was that there's no way this idiot was smart enough to pull this off by himself. Would he even be able to count the money to see if the amount was correct?

He stopped and looked at me cross-eyed and then down at the black leather bag I'd transferred the money into. I nodded as if to say, "That's the money, idiot." He stared at me, then coldly threw a white envelope toward me, grabbed the bag, and started to haul ass through the park.

He almost bumped into Cisco, who was sitting on a bike, shirtless, drinking from a bottle of water looking like just an ordinary guy out in the park for an early evening ride.

So this was the guy who'd turned my life upside down? I shook my head in disbelief and watched the rich evening sunset cover the city. I let out a deep breath, glad that this episode of *The Streets of New Orleans* was over. I could now head home and get ready for my trip to Phoenix. For the first time in weeks, I was going to be able to enjoy my time with Dray.

I walked a few feet toward the lamppost where Cisco was stationed when I bumped into a woman who was quickly rounding the corner without looking where she was going. When I turned to apologize, there was a moment of instant recognition. Her face was a little fatter and I almost didn't recognize her, yet I knew who she was. Those olive-green eyes were just as cold and her styleless bleached-blonde hair just as messy as when I spotted her at the mall. Still, it didn't make sense. What was she doing here?

Confused, I asked, "Do I know you?"

She had a look of deep loathing yet at the same time a self-satisfied smile on her face. "You know me, asshole," she said with an icy tone that matched her eyes.

She was obviously pregnant, with a pumpkinlike stomach sticking out of her yellow Empire dress. What in the hell was Judi doing in this park, giving me so much shade?

"Who are you?" I asked, trying not to let on I knew exactly who she was.

"Stop playing, Aldridge. You know damn well who I am. I'm your boyfriend's fucking wife, you little idiot."

"My boyfriend?"

"Cut the crap."

"Who are you talking about?"

"Drayton Jones. You know who that is?"

"Yes I know Dray, but he's a friend. So you're his wife? Nice to meet you," I said extending my hand.

She brushed it away and said, "You think you're cute."

"I haven't a clue as to what you are talking about. What are you doing here all alone?"

"Just making sure that our transaction came off without a hitch, and to give you my own personal message," she said with a steely directness.

"What are you talking about?" Was this *bitch* behind all this shit?

"I'm talking about you and my husband. If you don't want your D.C. escapades broadcast all over the world, then you will leave him alone and I mean for good. We are getting ready to start a family and we don't need your ass in the picture." She moved in closer. "You better be glad that I let you keep some of Dray's money, but if you contact him in any way from this moment forward, I will take it all from you. That would be very easy for me to do. I'm his wife, not some pathetic faggot boyfriend he keeps on the side. That money belongs to me anyway. Do I make myself clear?"

As crazy as this episode had been up until now, never had it been crazier. My heart hammered away in my chest and I took a deep breath before speaking. "I don't know what you're talking about," I said, making eye contact with Cisco. I wanted to let him know that I wasn't in any danger but I still needed him close by.

"Don't be coy and cute with me, Aldridge. Or should I call you AJ? Yeah, I think I will. I knew all about your little affair before I married Dray but figured it would end when we left Atlanta. You're not dealing with some sista girl," she said, snapping her fingers in mockery, "who's too stupid to not know that the man she was about to marry had a boy on the side. But I will say this for you, AJ: you're persistent, so I had to deal with you the way my daddy deals with his business partners, and that means hitting you in your wallet." She stepped closer to me and raised her jeweled finger and waved. "Do not contact Dray under any circumstances or not only will I release your little sex tape on the

Internet, but I will put your sick phone conversations and texts on full blast. Then for the pièce de résistance I'll tell Dray's parents about all this madness. And we both know they would be crushed and so would Dray. So if you love him like you say you do, then it's time you show it."

So this is what everything came down to. Some cheap blonde who managed to trap Dray called the shots for the guy who loved Dray with all his heart. At the same time, I didn't know what made me madder — that this woman was giving orders or that Dray had settled for such a low-down piece of trash. He'd never spoken of her in anything but adoring terms, so maybe Judi would make a fine actress.

I didn't respond, but a silent rage started to warm my body. I wanted to slap the shit out of this woman, but I could flash forward and see my ass sitting in a jail cell for hitting a pregnant woman, and a white one at that.

"So do I make myself clear? I don't want to have this conversation again. I need my husband to turn his full attention to me, our child, and the few good years he might have left to make millions. You understand me?"

Recalling my promise to Dray never to reveal our relationship, I said, "I don't know what you're talking about."

Although she flashed a fake smile, I could tell she was not amused. "So that's how you're going to play it? Well, let me leave you with this piece of advice: if you dare to get on that plane to Arizona tonight, you're bringing Dray's life, as he knows it, to an end. I'll be on the phone to Mississippi so fast that his family will think another Katrina has hit."

I'd had all I could take. "Nice seeing you, Judi. I hope the rest of your pregnancy is a stress-free one."

"I can live stress-free as long as you do what I say and have no further contact with Dray. And if you think for the slightest second that I'm not serious about doing what I just said, then you are sadly mistaken."

I turned around and realized that Cisco was now only a few feet from us. I guess the conversation had gone on long enough to signal trouble.

"Is everything all right?" Cisco interjected.

Judi turned in disgust. "Who is this? What kind of person are you? Are you two-timing my husband with somebody else's husband?"

"Aldridge, is everything cool?" Cisco asked again.

"Everything is cool. Are you ready to roll?" I shot Judi my death look, warning her that she'd fucked with the wrong guy. She might have had the upper hand right now, but that could change at any moment. I wasn't going to roll over that easily.

As I started to walk out of the park, she shouted, "Don't force me to make those phone calls, Aldridge, because I will. Nobody messes with Judi Ledbetter and just walks away. Do you hear me? Nobody!"

When we were safely out of the park, Cisco asked if I wanted to talk about what had just happened.

"I really don't want to get into it right now."

"That's cool, but who was that pregnant white chick and why was she all up in your grill like that?"

I turned to face him. "I said I don't want to talk about it."

Cisco let it go and we walked a few blocks in silence. My nerves had calmed some and I had the urge to tell him what had gone on, as much to process my anger as to share the whole story.

"That was my boi's wife, and it seems like she's the one who's been blackmailing both of us." There, it was out in the open at last. Since I wasn't going to see Dray anymore, I had no need to protect our secrets. Judi was the kind of low-class bitch who would tell his father and Dray would never forgive me, knowing I could have prevented that.

"How did she find out about you two? You guys are together, right?"

"Yeah, we're together. Have been for seven years." I was surprised at how easily I released the secret I'd kept for years.

"But how did she find out about it?" Cisco asked.

"I guess that's the million-dollar question."

We turned onto a street. "Are you going to tell him what happened?"

"Nope."

"Then who was that dude who left with the money?"

"Someone Judi paid to do her dirty work. But taking my money, my boi, and my house wasn't enough. When she saw me, she couldn't resist letting me know she knew what the deal was," I said.

"Bitches all the same no matter what color they are."

I didn't need to hear that and was relieved to reach my town house where I could finally be alone.

"True. Good looking-out."

"No problem. Do you want me to come inside and make sure everything is cool?"

"I think everything will be fine. I really appreciate your concern, but I got some things

I need to take care of. Give me a call tomorrow and we can talk about resuming my workouts."

"That's what's up." Cisco surprised me by lunging forward and giving me a brotherman hug. He slapped my shoulder by way of saying goodbye, then climbed on his bike.

I turned the key to my door and watched Cisco disappear into the New Orleans night.

For the first time in a week, I walked into my house without dreading some danger that might await me. Strange as it seems, I felt safer knowing who the enemy was. I picked up the phone and called my cell phone provider, canceling my three cell phones. I got a new cell phone number but made sure that it was private. I confirmed twice with the customer service representative that no one would be able to gain access.

"No one can get it unless you give it to them," she assured me.

Next I called my mother and gave her my new number. When she asked if everything was okay, I lied and told her yes. I explained that I was getting too many telemarketing calls in the middle of meetings. I promised to try my best to make it home in two months for Christmas.

I called Jade but got her voice mail. "Hey

Jade, I'm taking off for a couple of weeks and I had to change my phone numbers. Don't worry about me. I promise to reach out once things settle down a bit."

I then phoned Maurice. I knew I couldn't hang around New Orleans for long and would have to find a place to stay for a couple of days. I needed to be around a good friend as I figured out what I would do next. Of all people, he knew how it felt to lose a man.

"Come on, child, I could use the company," Maurice said.

"Are you sure it won't be a problem?"

"If it gets to be a problem, then I'll put your ass out," he joked.

"I think I'll leave here first thing tomorrow."

"Does this have anything to do with the phantom boyfriend?"

At first I began to resort to the usual lies to cover my tracks, but to my surprise I said, "Up until now everything had to do with the phantom, but not anymore. Not anymore." Just speaking the truth so spontaneously felt like a new beginning in some small way.

"I'm glad to hear that, child. I'm sure he wasn't good enough for you. Men ain't shit. Never have been, never will be. It's all about the dick for them. That's real talk, honey."

As Maurice continued to ramble on about how lucky I was to be rid of my boyfriend, I felt a deep regret rise within me. I had an aching sense of sorrow. I felt like I had lived most of my adult life in a dream. A dream that died that evening in the park with Judi. Now I had to go and live in the real world. And my friend Maurice was as real as it got.

TWENTY-THREE

I woke up to what was going to be my last day in New Orleans for a while. I'd not spoken to Dray since the drop-off and I struggled with my tremendous feeling of loss. With my phone shut off and him on the road and unable to just drop in on me, I pictured him deeply concerned. At least I hoped he was worried. More than anything, I imagined he was pissed.

Morning had settled in cool and secure, a mild drizzle falling outside the bedroom window. I got out of bed and emptied the contents of my closets into three suitcases I had lined up on the floor. The stuff that didn't fit in the suitcases I put in two big boxes to give to the local Salvation Army. I'd loved shopping for all those clothes, yet it was surprisingly easy to let them go. After all, I reminded myself, they're just clothes.

As I packed, I was overcome with flashes of anger at what Judi was doing to Dray and I fantasized about getting revenge. I desperately wanted to get the bitch back, but she had me over a barrel.

I thought about calling Dray and telling him what had happened and giving him an ultimatum. I knew he loved me, but was that enough to give him the courage to face his fans and, more important, his family? Was that asking for too much?

Then I thought how selfish I sounded by thinking this little love affair was more important than Dray's career and family. He would never forgive me if I forced him to make that decision, and so leaving and following Judi's orders was most likely the wise move.

Just as I was going into the kitchen to get something to drink there was a knock at the door. What if it was Dray? What explanation would I give him about the suitcases? I wouldn't put it past Judi to show up at my door for round two. I walked into the living room and through the side window looked outside and saw Jade.

Relieved, I opened the door.

"What are you doing here?"

"I got your message. What is going on?" Jade asked with a look of genuine concern. "You can't take off just like that."

"Everything is fine," I said.

"But where are you going?"

"Atlanta, to help out a friend of mine."

"Is he or she sick?"

"No, just dealing with a little love issue."

"Oh, he's got the love jones," Jade said, understanding in a snap.

"Yeah, I guess you could call it that."

"Is it your friend Maurice that you were telling me about?"

"What about Maurice?" I asked.

"Is he the one in love?"

How had she remembered his name? I couldn't have mentioned him more than twice, but I guess women remember insignificant shit like that.

"Yeah," I stuttered. I appreciated her concern but was in no mood for company all of a sudden.

"Are you sure?"

"Sure about what?"

"Are you sure no one is messing with you?"

"Why would you ask me that?"

"I don't know. I just have a funny feeling," Jade said vaguely.

"Trust me, Jade, everything will be fine."

"Do you need me to take care of things while you're away?"

I hadn't gotten around to that. "Yeah, Jade. Thanks a lot. I'll pay you when I get back. I hope that's okay."

"I'm not worried about that. I just hope everything is all right and you can get back here soon. Besides, I think my ship is getting ready to come in."

There it was again. It was as if she knew a whole lot more than she was saying.

"What's going on?"

"Oh, nothing," Jade said quickly. "Just make sure you call me when you get settled."

"I will." I couldn't shake the feeling that something was strange with Jade changing the subject. I asked, "What do you have planned today?"

"I have a couple of in-home appointments and I'm going to try and get to the gym."

"Okay, give me a hug and I'll see you soon," I said as I moved close to Jade and hugged her tightly. Just before I released her, she whispered, "You know I'm here if you need me."

"I know," I said as slow, small tears formed in my eyes.

After meeting with a real estate agent to put my place on the market, I took one final look around the living room and my eyes landed on the phone. I knew it would be cut off soon, but I suddenly had the urge to make a call.

I was relieved when I heard a dial tone and

I immediately began dialing. After a few rings there was the familiar voice that always brought a smile to my face.

"Bella," I said.

"AJ, I was just thinking about you!"

"What were you thinking?"

"How I couldn't wait to see you again."

"And I can't wait to see you, sweetheart. Is Mama at home?"

"Yes, she's in the kitchen cooking, I think. You want to speak with her?"

"Yes, darling."

"Okay," Bella said.

"I love you, Bella Lynn."

"I love you too."

As I waited for my mother to come to the phone, I thought about how lucky I was to have my mother and sister in my life. I didn't want to admit it, but I was going to need them more than ever as I worked my way through this nightmare of a breakup. I wasn't about to dump the whole mess in their laps, but Mama was smart enough and knew me so well that I wouldn't have to say much for her to get the general idea.

"Hey, baby," my mother said. "Is everything all right?"

"I guess so," I said somberly.

My mother could always tell from my voice how I was feeling and so I guess it had betrayed me again.

"It will be soon."

"Is there something special I can do? Do you need me to come to New Orleans?"

"No. I just called to tell you I'll be in Atlanta for a couple of weeks."

My mama was no fool. "What's wrong, baby?"

"Oh, Mama, I'll be all right." I paused to consider what I was about to say. "I just need you to pray for me."

"I always do. You know that. I don't know why you would even ask me."

"I know you do, but I might need extra prayers the next couple of months."

"Does this have anything to do with your special relationship?"

It was as if she'd struck a nerve. I suddenly felt tears running down my face. "Yeah," I mumbled. "It does."

"Do you mind me asking what happened?"

"There's too much to go into, but it's over and that makes me really sad," I said. Mama didn't know the half of it.

"Have you been crying?"

"Yes," I said.

"Baby, let me give you a little piece of advice that my mother gave me the first time a boy broke my heart. I want you to hear this, so first stop crying."

I wiped the tears with the back of my hand and asked my mother what my grandmother had said.

"Don't cry because it's over. Smile because it happened."

TWENTY-FOUR

Christmas Day arrived in Atlanta, cold and wet. The city needed the rain, but I didn't need the gloomy weather to take me further into a love hangover — no, make that a depression. Leaving Dray hurt just as much today as it had when I made the seven-hour drive to Atlanta.

Maurice had told me the night before Christmas that he hoped the holidays would help snap me out of my funk in time so I could enjoy the New Year. Besides, he said, he didn't want his best friend carrying doom and gloom to his Christmas dinner. He had invited about thirty of his friends over for a huge Christmas dinner catered by S.T.E.P.S., an event-planning company that hosted most of Atlanta's elite affairs. I guess business had picked up for Maurice because he wasn't cutting any corners this Christmas. Or maybe he was still auditioning people for his big party.

I admired the way he poured his heart into his design firm, party planning, and everything he attempted. Failure was not a part of his vocabulary.

Maurice had hired someone to decorate his ranch-style home in Jonesboro with lights and pageantry outside as well as inside. When I woke up Christmas morning, the chef was busy preparing dinner, but he wasn't too busy to make omelets and fresh blueberry muffins for Maurice and me.

"I hope you're not going to walk around here all day with that long face," Maurice said as he took a sip of hot apple cider. The breakfast nook where we sat was full of the cider's delicious aroma.

"You know the real reason I'm having this little Christmas party, don't you?" Maurice asked as he took a pinch of his muffin and smiled a sly grin.

"Because it's Christmas and you love giving parties."

"Yes, that's true, but my list for the big party isn't where it needs to be. Still way too many people, and so I need to make some cuts before the New Year. So I invited some people who are at the bottom of the list and might find themselves with no invite or on the waiting list. You can help me make cuts. Won't that be fun?"

"I don't know if I'd be good at that," I said, wondering how Maurice took pleasure in cutting out people who were about to be his guests at Christmas dinner.

"Don't worry about that. I'll teach you. Pay close attention to their conversation and wardrobe. If they can't dress well for the holidays, then there is no hope."

"Do they know that they're being judged today?"

"Child, boo. They don't have a clue. A couple of them have already been telling people they're in."

I didn't say anything for a couple of moments as Maurice rambled on about the Christmas party and the big one for Labor Day. Every now and then I heard him call out names and say things like, "Make sure you watch her because she can be shady." Finally I broke from my trance and said what I was thinking.

"I know, I should have gone to North Carolina, but I didn't want my mother to worry about me," I said.

"I still don't know what happened, and I know you're never going to tell me, but there's a new year coming, Aldridge. You need to try to put whatever happened in New Orleans behind you and start the year out right," Maurice said. "You deserve some real happiness."

"I think finding a new place to live will be the first thing I'll do," I said.

"Well, you picked the right time. It's a buyer's market. I'm going to buy some of the foreclosures in Midtown and rent them out."

"With the economy being so weak, you sure are doing well," I said, taking a bite from a muffin.

Maurice smiled, obviously satisfied with his life. "Yeah, things have picked up, but that's because I haven't limited myself to decorating houses. You know me, boi, I'm always working on a bigger plan," Maurice said.

"That's smart."

"Go spruce yourself up, child. Maybe Santa left you a new outfit and you'll meet your next boyfriend today."

"I promise not to be a drag on your party. I'm almost looking forward to it. It's been so long since I've been on my own at Christmas," I said. I couldn't help but remember the Christmases Dray and I had spent in various cities. Usually there wasn't a game on Christmas Day, but if they had an away game the next day, the team would arrive on Christmas Day. Dray always had several gifts for me. The thing about Dray was that although he was preoccupied and demanding, he still paid attention. One year he gave me a Rolex watch with 13 on it, his jersey number and the date we met, simply because, he said, he knew it would make me smile. We used to talk about the day when we would be able to spend Christmas together in our own home. For the longest time, I held on to this hope and truthfully I think Dray did too. Neither of us knew how or when this would come about, but we held out hope. Now that was never going to happen and I needed to give up that dream. But that was not going to happen overnight.

The Hornets had a game in New Orleans the day after Christmas, so I knew Dray was spending the day with *her.* Having come face to face with Judi in such an ugly way, I couldn't begin to guess how he could stand to look at her at all, much less start a family. From the beginning I couldn't understand what he saw in her, and now it was impossible to even guess.

I wasn't looking forward to my return to New Orleans the next week, but there was a buyer for the town house and I needed to be there to supervise the packing of my prized paintings. The realtor thought leaving them up would help speed up the sale.

I sat watching yet another Christmas parade on television in Maurice's guest room when I heard the first few guests arrive. One of them broke out with a loud "Girl, you got Christmas up in here in this camp for sure!" which set my back up. Even in the best of times, I didn't know if I was ready for a bunch of queens on Christmas, much less now that I was mending a broken heart. I'd promised Maurice I wouldn't be a drag, so I told myself to pull it together.

I moved through the kitchen and dining room and tried to give polite smiles and nods to the guests. They all appeared to be black gay men in their thirties and forties, handsomely dressed, but there were definitely too many Christmas ensembles with dangling handkerchiefs. From first glance, Maurice wouldn't have a hard time getting his invitation list down. Damn, I was starting to sound like his best friend.

They stared at me approvingly, as if I were a gift who'd just jumped out of a box. Having older men cruising me was the last thing I had on my mind, so I excused myself and moved back into the kitchen.

The Christmas spread looked like it was ready to be photographed for a food magazine. There were two golden-brown turkeys, a standing rib roast, and a honey-baked ham in the center of the table. Bowls of macaroni and cheese, candied yams, dressing, rolls, cornbread, and salad completed the feast. There were two handsome waiters in tuxes attending to the food and ready to serve the all-male dinner party.

By 3:00 all the guests had arrived. They seemed to know one another, giving warm hugs and kisses as each entered the room. It had been ages since I'd been alone with so many gay men, even longer since I'd been to a gay dinner party. I felt like an outsider in a room full of men you would think I would have had so much in common with. Maurice moved from one guest to the next with a bottle of champagne, refilling empty glasses as he went. Little did these poor fools know they were being judged by their host.

I noticed his ease with gay men and thought about how I never quite got on with them, not even in the beginning, when I was young and just coming out. I seldom saw myself reflected in that new gay world, and when I did it was usually some silly snap queen who had nothing in common with me other than being another black man who preferred sex with men. It made choosing as my partners men who didn't identify as gay but slept with men that much easier.

Watching the genuine fondness these guys at the dinner party displayed openly and un-ambiguously for each other, I felt tenderness for them, for the tough path any black gay man had to walk. But as much as I was touched by their camaraderie, I couldn't quite reach it. Their world and the one Dray and I lived in were as different as South Dakota and South Beach. I imagined what Dray would say walking into this scene, and I smiled without intending to. He'd have felt as out of place here as at a bridal shower.

Looking for a place to hide out and watch a game, I located a television in the study. I soon found myself thinking only about Dray as I watched the Miami Heat compete against the Cleveland Cavaliers. I was slightly amused as LeBron James's mother was interviewed and revealed to the national television audience that she'd purchased some diamond cuff links for her son, but only after his stylist had approved them. I thought of two Christmases before, when I'd purchased the exact same thing for Dray and how happy he was with them. When he opened the black velvet box, he was so excited that he couldn't wait to slip them into his shirt and model them for me.

Maurice came into the room looking a lot less festive.

"Well, making the cut is going to be easier than I thought. I can't believe the nerve of that bitch," he said, still holding the green champagne bottle. "Sloane Mouton came to my party. That bitch was not invited. If he thinks he going to get an invitation to my party, then the bitch is crazier than I thought. And trust me, I'm going to have top-notch security there."

"Who is that?"

"This guy who I went out with a few times. Everything seemed great, but then he just stopped calling me without explanation. He wouldn't return my calls either. I heard he was trying to hit on Tay, so I guess he was looking for a sugar daddy. But I got his ass. I had all his utilities cut off and tried to cancel his credit cards, but I realized the bitch most likely didn't have any. I don't know if he knows I did it, but I paid his ass back good," Maurice fumed.

"Did he come with someone?"

Maurice poured himself more champagne. I hoped he didn't get drunk or else this party could take a nasty turn.

"His new boyfriend, Lyon, who I invited only because I was going to make a play for him, or at the very least have him as eye candy for the Labor Day party. Lyon didn't mention he had a boyfriend. I should throw both of their asses out. Lyon may have just got cut from the list even if he fine as hell."

"It's Christmas and this is your party. Just

ignore them and enjoy the rest of your guests."

Maurice thought about what I'd said, let out a deep theatrical sigh, and rejoined his guests.

After the game was over, I switched off the television and contemplated returning to the party. I got as far as the hallway, where I overheard one of the conversations. Of course they were whispering about who would get an invitation to the big party. Several men were talking about the movies: *Dirty Laundry,* a rare black gay family comedy starring the straight hunk Rockmond Dunbar, and the new Denzel Washington movie *The Great Debaters,* which Oprah Winfrey produced and promoted heavily on her talk show. One guy mentioned the new Will Smith movie and how much money it had made, and how Will was now one of the hottest male stars in Hollywood.

Eavesdropping further, I heard from another corner of the room, "We taking over, child, and if Obama wins this election, white folks are going to be heading back to England."

I casually entered the den, trying not to appear aloof but not wanting to get drawn into a conversation either. I also dodged the heavy cruising taking place right and left. It felt strange being young and single again. As depressed as I was over the breakup, realizing that I was a good-looking young guy with his whole life ahead brought me hope suddenly. I grabbed a handful of almonds from the side table and paused when I heard the subject of football come up. A couple of guys spoke about how dreadful the Atlanta Falcons were and how their coach had recently bolted the team to coach the University of Arkansas. I heard them say it was all Michael Vick's fault, but they admitted they missed seeing the handsome black man leading the home team and lamented that Vick had played his last game in an Atlanta Falcons uniform.

A few minutes later, the dinner bell rang and Maurice summoned his guests to the dining room for a moment of giving thanks. We all stood around the huge maple table holding hands as he led his guests in prayer. I wondered which of these guys were Lyon and the new boyfriend. As Maurice went on and on like he was delivering a sermon, I snuck a peek at the tree and noticed about thirty blue Tiffany boxes under it. Now this was big-time, and I could only imagine what the parting gifts would be come September. If Mo was living this good, then maybe I could make it on my own in Atlanta too.

When Maurice finally finished, the chorus of amens that followed sounded more like sighs of relief than blessings.

In spite of the glamour of the affair, this wasn't a formal sit-down dinner. The table couldn't possibly have accommodated the large number of guests, so an elegant buffet with servers had been set up. I fixed myself a plate and then retreated to the study. I said a prayer of my own that nobody would miss or join me. I sat all alone watching another basketball game.

For about twenty minutes, it seemed my prayers were answered. I was relieved that I wouldn't be stuck at a table between chatty dinner companions. Then a tall, slender man with a plate in his hand walked into the study. Damn, how did he know I was there?

"What are you doing in here all by yourself?" he asked playfully.

"Just watching the game," I said politely, but with as little enthusiasm as possible.

"Mind if I join you?" he asked.

"Come on in," I said, gesturing to a leather chair to my left.

He sat down and for a minute or two ate in silence, all the while surveying the room like he was sizing up the place for an estate auction.

"Who's playing?" he asked.

"The Lakers."

"That's Kobe's team, right?"

"Kobe plays for the Lakers," I said, overemphasizing the obvious. I kept my eyes glued to the television, hoping he'd take a hint.

"I'm Bobby. Bobby Lee," he said, offering his hand. "Are you Mo's new roommate?"

"I'm his houseguest. My name is Aldridge," I said, shaking his hand.

"Nice meeting you, Aldridge. So what do you think of Atlanta?"

"I've lived here before," I said.

He gently dug into the food on his plate. "What brought you back?"

"I haven't decided if I'm coming back," I said.

"Where are you from originally?"

"North Carolina," I said, between bites, intentionally trying to sound noncommittal.

"Wow, me too. I'm from Gaston. What city are you from?"

"Raleigh."

"Isn't that funny — the first new person I meet at this little affair is one of my homeboys." Bobby laughed.

"Yeah, funny," I said, trying to refocus my attention on the game. I didn't want to hurt this guy's feelings, but all I wanted was to be left alone.

"I don't guess you're worried about getting an invitation to Maurice's big party, since you living with him."

"That's not the way it is," I said defensively.

"I heard he's not inviting a lot of the people here today. Is that true?"

"I don't know anything about the guest list."

"Oh. Can you believe New York is going to marry Tailor Made?"

"What?"

"Don't you watch the show *I Love New York?*"

"No, what's that?" I asked.

"It's a reality show about this girl whose nickname is New York. At first New York was on that show with that ugly-ass Flavor Flav and he broke her heart twice, and then she got her own show and the guy broke her heart. This year I was expecting her to fall in love with this fine-ass brother she had on the show, but she picked the white boy. Now they say they getting married. Ain't that some crazy-ass shit?" Bobby smiled.

"I wouldn't know. I've never seen the show," I repeated.

"It's like watching a train wreck," he said, shaking his head between bites. "Once you take a peek, you can't look away."

I leaned in closer to the television. "Whatever," I said. Hopefully Bobby would go and refill his plate.

There was an awkward silence, which I was actually grateful for.

"Who do you think has a better chance to be president? Hillary or Obama?"

"Neither one," I said. "We'll get another white man."

"You think so?"

"I know so," I said matter-of-factly.

"Do you like sports or do you watch for the cute boys?"

"I like sports," I snapped.

"I like the cute boys, but I don't like basketball so much with the long baggy shorts. I miss the good ol' days when they wore hot pants." Bobby laughed to himself.

If he wasn't going to leave, then I would. "If you will excuse me, I think I'm going to the kitchen to get some more food," I said.

"Do you mind bringing me a turkey leg and a little dressing? Oh, some gravy too," he said.

I wanted to ask him if I looked like a member of the waitstaff, but instead I told him it would be a while before I came back.

"Don't worry, I'm not going anywhere," Bobby said with a wink, eyeing me up and down like only a gay in heat can do.

I didn't go back for refills but instead went into my room and closed the door. After a short nap brought on by a case of "itis," as my mother liked to call it, I walked into the kitchen to find Maurice paying the caterer in cash. That looked like a lot of cash to have lying around, but leave it to Maurice to get the best deal by paying cash and holding out the carrot of possibly getting the contract for his big event.

"You did a great job," he told the caterer, a big man with a full beard dressed in a white chef's coat. "Everything Lou said about you was true. The best in Atlanta."

"Thank you. I left some extra cards on the counter, and please tell your friends about me. And I'd like to put in a bid for your Labor Day party."

"Of course you would," Maurice said. "And doing this party for a little over cost certainly makes you the front-runner."

"I'm glad to hear that. I've heard a lot about your plans."

"But not everything, I hope. I still got some surprises up my Dolce & Gabbana sleeves," Maurice said with a hearty laugh.

As far as I could tell, all the guests had cleared out. I went to the refrigerator to get a glass of pomegranate juice, which Maurice had convinced me was even healthier than green tea. This alluring scarlet fruit juice actually made me feel like it was stopping the aging process.

"So where did you disappear to?" Maurice stood with his hands on his hips, giving me a reproachful eye. "I looked around and you'd gone ghost."

I located the juice in a plastic jug, hiding behind the leftovers in large aluminum trays.

"The food gave me a case of the 'itis' and I needed a nap," I said.

"A case of what?"

"The 'itis,' as in prefaced by the n-word. That's what my mother calls it."

Maurice rolled his eyes. "So did you meet anybody you like?"

"Nope, I sure didn't," I said, hoping this would put an end to the subject.

"Did you *try?* What about Bobby? I saw you talking to him."

I turned and faced him. "Bobby, you're kidding, right, Mo? I told you I'm not ready to start another relationship."

Maurice placed his hand on my shoulder. "Who said anything about a relationship? Because that's not what I asked. You better locate you a friend with benefits or a nice piece of trade, because winter is upon us, child, and you don't want to sleep in that basement room all by yourself."

"I'll be all right," I said solemnly. My thoughts immediately went back to happier times with Dray. I'd struggled like hell to put him out of my thoughts, but that would take time.

"Are you thinking about him?" Maurice asked.

"Who?"

"Whoever you left or who left you."

"Not really. Well, maybe I was thinking about him just a little," I said.

Maurice poured himself a cup of coffee from the pot on the stove. "Look, Aldridge, I know you might be hurting now, but time will change all that. If this guy wasn't good enough for you to introduce him to your best friend . . . well, he just couldn't be that special."

I thought about what Maurice had said, and gulped down the juice. "Maybe you're right."

"I'm always right, doll, but I thought you knew that."

TWENTY-FIVE

It was New Year's Day, and while many use the day as a jump-off point for new beginnings, I couldn't seem to get out of bed. The house was empty because Maurice had decided on a whim to take a few friends of his down to the Dominican Republic for a week of sun and being chased and serviced by handsome Dominican men. I'm sure some more party cuts would be made as well. He had invited me to join them, but I wasn't interested in a trip for sex and sun. Actually, I looked forward to the opportunity of having the house to myself.

I dragged myself out of bed and over to the television. The E! channel had on its end-of-the-year review, and when they came to the part where they showed pictures of the many celebrities who had died during the year, I wondered how many of them, if any, knew a year ago that last year would be the beginning of the end for them. Damn, that was a morbid thought, AJ, I told myself.

But if anyone knew firsthand what a difference a year could make, it was me. I was of course missing Dray and remembering the times we spent cuddled up in bed watching the marathon of college bowl games. It wasn't that I loved football so much, but spending all that leisure time in bed with Dray made up some of the happiest moments of our relationship.

I'd been gone from New Orleans for a couple of months and pictured Dray frantic about my sudden disappearance. He might even have thought I died, but of course wouldn't go to the police. I thought about dropping him a note to say not to worry, that I was okay, but thought Judi might find out and deliver on her promise.

Imagining Dray calling the hospitals to see if I'd been in an accident made missing him all the sadder. People don't walk out on a relationship when they're happy; they do it when they want out, like my dad. Poor Dray was probably going through hell worrying about me, and he could thank his loving wife for that.

I hadn't been outside, but I could tell by the coldness of the wood floor against my bare feet that it was a typical January day. I loved the solitude of an empty house and was reminded that I needed to find a place of my own.

I decided right there that I would go to New Orleans immediately. Enough lying around and doing nothing. I was going to see how the sale of the house was coming along — more specifically, when I might expect the cash I would need to buy another house.

I pulled a couple of pairs of slacks and a couple of shirts from the small guest-room closet and grabbed some warm-ups and enough underwear for four days. When I got ready to pack my shitload of toiletries and sneakers, I suddenly remembered that the bag I used to carry them in was probably somewhere at the bottom of the Mississippi River, most likely discarded by Judi's henchman.

I started to head for Lenox Mall to pick up a new duffel bag but didn't really feel like going all that way and dealing with the crowds returning unwanted Christmas gifts, so instead I went into Maurice's bedroom to see if he'd left something I might borrow. I was sure he wouldn't mind and I planned to return before he did.

I opened the door to his bedroom and peeked around the door like I was expecting Maurice to be sitting there lounging on his chair.

The room was immaculate and decorated in sort of a masculine Laura Ashley that combined bold floral patterns with touches of leather, like the trunk that sat at the foot of the bed.

There was a new forty-six-inch flat-screen television on the wall above a maple dresser and pictures of Maurice's family and one or two old boyfriends. There were stacks of books with samples of invitations Maurice had spent hours looking over for his party, and stacks of comps of male models applying for spots as eye candy for the big bash.

The door to his large walk-in closet was slightly ajar and I figured this was the place Maurice might keep any luggage. I noticed a set of Louis Vuitton bags that I'd never seen him carry or brag about and figured it belonged to one of his friends, so I decided not to even touch it.

The closet, like the room, was well organized and had the feel of a color-coordinated sock-and-T-shirt store. I was almost afraid to touch anything for fear of messing up his stuff. In the corner of the closet, I spotted a couple of black leather luggage pieces and thought I was in luck.

The first one I saw other than the LV bags was a large leather bag the size and shape of a hatbox. Not exactly the piece I was looking for, but I pulled the top off to see how deep it was.

To my surprise there were various snapshots of young African American men in various stages of undress. Some were strangely sexy while a few were downright pornographic. Looking more closely at a few of the pictures, I decided I was intruding, so I closed the hatbox quickly.

I found an even bigger surprise when I opened the second leather bag. Instead of containing pictures, it had stacks of new hundred-dollar bills. Maybe this was money from donors for his party, but still I wondered what the hell Maurice was thinking. Surely he knew how dangerous it was to leave all that money lying around his place, especially with the rough trade he liked going in and out of his house at times.

It was way too much cash to leave around, especially considering the type of thug boy Maurice sometimes kept company with. I wondered if he was involved in some illegal cash-only venture or just wanted to keep his money close to him. It suddenly looked like I would be heading out to Lenox after all. I hoped that all the pissed-off people with bad gifts and the bargain shoppers were taking a break or had run out of money.

TWENTY-SIX

I snuck back into New Orleans like a fugitive. I took a hotel room at the Hyatt Place Hotel, about thirty miles outside the city in a small town called Slidell.

I didn't venture into the city until the Friday after New Year's Day. Part of my choosing the remote location was because I didn't want to risk the chance of running into Judi or Dray, but also because all the decent hotels in the city were booked solid with the both the Sugar Bowl and the National Championship football games being played in the Superdome.

The only person I told was Jade, who had invited me to a chicken dinner at Willie Mae's Scotch House. It seemed like a safe bet since Dray wasn't big on fried food and I certainly couldn't see Judi having her ass up in the joint.

The place was packed, and we had to wait about forty-five minutes before we were seated. I didn't mind because it gave Jade and me a chance to catch up. She looked good and it appeared she'd added a few more tracks of hair to her well-kept weave.

"So," she began. "Two weeks turn into two months for you. What were you doing all that time? It looks like you lost weight. Have you been eating right?"

"I've been trying to lose some weight," I said.

"Sure you have." Jade laughed.

We were finally seated and handed menus.

"I must have a ton of mail."

"Got it right here," Jade said, reaching into a black leather bag. She handed me two stacks of mail held together by a rubber band.

"Thanks," I said.

"Now tell me again why you aren't staying at your fabulous place?" Jade asked suspiciously.

"I'm selling it and I don't want to be there when they bring in new owners. Might cost myself a sale if they see my black ass sitting up in there."

"I heard that." She laughed.

"Speaking of black, can you believe Obama won the Iowa caucus?"

"That was a shock. Do you think he can really win?" Jade asked.

"One day, but I still think we get a white boy this time."

"You ain't said nothing but the truth. All people need to do before they vote is to pay a visit down here. I know you read about how our kinfolks acted when they announced they were tearing down the housing projects."

"Yeah, I have mixed emotions about that. I'm still hoping to work with Brad Pitt's project, doing what I can."

"How is it going? I saw something on television about him the other day."

"I can actually see progress being made. It's really wonderful what he's doing. His people say families may be moving into the new homes before the end of the year."

"I'm surprised I haven't run into him. I usually run into famous people. Used to happen to me all the time when I lived in Los Angeles."

The restaurant was buzzing with conversation. Fortunately Jade and I had been seated at a small table, so we didn't have to shout to hear each other.

"Are you still working hard?" I asked.

"I guess you could say, 'Hardly working.' I was able to give up my waitress gig but I still do a few facials and massages here and there," Jade said. "I met someone and he takes pretty good care of me."

"Who? Reggie Bush? Did you finally meet him?"

"It's not Reggie but I did meet him. Reggie at last!" she said sarcastically. "Not quite what I was expecting. He's short and I think he doesn't have much love for brown sugar."

"Don't they all," I said with a smirk.

"That's why I found myself a basketball player."

"A basketball player? Who?" I asked, wondering if it was somebody I knew. Wondering if it was someone Dray knew.

"He doesn't live in New Orleans, so I might be moving to Cleveland."

"Is it LeBron James?" I asked excitedly.

"Ain't he married? Miss Jade don't do married anymore, baby. No, it's not him, but it's one of his teammates. I went to a Hornets game because one of my clients gave me tickets. My seat was with the wives, so I was sitting right behind the Cavaliers bench."

"So how did you meet him?"

Jade took a sip of her water.

"I was minding my own business, but I noticed him checking me out. I was dressed in a pale pink pantsuit and of course the pants were hugging my assets. So anyhoo, when I was leaving, this young guy runs me down saying that somebody on the Cavaliers asked me to wait for him outside the locker room. I knew it was him and I didn't have shit else to do, so I took a chance and waited to see what he was talking about."

"What happened next?"

"We went out for cocktails. I liked his talk and the next week I was on a flight to Cleveland. Just like that. And to think how I spent all that time chasing a man who don't even like my type." She grinned, recalling the meeting, and I sensed she enjoyed telling the story and finding the path to love.

I was so happy for Jade, but marveled at how differently the world played out for gay and straight people. I'd watched the wives section of the game countless times, feeling like I was as entitled as any of those women to be sitting there. But no matter how much I meant to Dray, that could never happen for me. I never kidded myself that it would, but hearing Jade's story and seeing how easy it was for a woman to step into a man's life and be accepted so quickly made her news a little bittersweet.

"What's his name?"

"Paul Peters," Jade said.

"Is he a brother?"

She frowned. "Of course he's a brother."

"How tall is he?"

"Six-five," Jade said proudly.

"What do you like about him?"

"He's crazy about me."

"That's good." I smiled. "What else?"

"He is sexy as fuck." Jade laughed.

"How so?" I asked, suddenly interested in sex once again, even though it was the straight kind.

"Let's just say he can get the panties off without raising my skirt," Jade said with a sexy wink.

I'm sure I blushed at that. "I'm so happy for you," I said. And I meant it too. Jade deserved her sexy basketball player. Even if I couldn't have mine, I was happy for Jade.

The waiter sat two sweet teas on the table and I looked at him and mouthed "Thank you."

"I'm happy for me too," Jade said. "Seems like my little blackmail paid off well for me."

My heart stopped for a second. "Blackmail? What are you talking about?"

"Well, the woman who gave me the tickets was one of my clients. Bitch never gave me the time of day. I would go out to her house, one of those brand-new mansions, and give her a facial and massage, and she wouldn't even look my way. Bitch thought she was all that. You know how white girls can be."

Jade picked up the menu for a moment and then put it right back down on the table.

I felt there had to be more to the story. "So come on, tell me what happened."

"It seems her husband plays for the Hornets. One day, when I had finished her facial and massage, I was in the bathroom off her master suite washing my hands. When I walked back out into her bedroom, she was on the phone, all frantic. She kept saying, 'Are you sure it's not my husband's? What happens if he can tell it's not his when the baby is born?' I thought to myself, Uh oh, this is some soap opera shit."

"What was she talking about?"

"The bitch is pregnant and her husband ain't the baby's daddy. I heard the entire shit. I wanted to turn and leave but I couldn't move. When she turned around and saw me standing there, you would have thought the bitch was looking at a ghost." Jade laughed at the memory.

"Is her husband white?" I asked, trying to think of the white players on the Hornets.

"No, that's the kicker. Her husband is black. She was fucking around with one of her husband's best friends on the team, and he's the daddy. But I think the friend is either white or real light-skinned. When she realized I'd heard her entire conversation, she basically admitted it to me and told me she'd do whatever I asked. It surprised me, because she came off as this really tough bitch for a white girl, but I guess she's out of her mind worried about her husband finding out he's not the baby's daddy."

For a moment I couldn't wrap my head around Jade's story. Could it be who I thought it was? Rather, who I prayed it might be? Certainly Judi couldn't be so stupid, I thought. I knew Dray was close to a couple of his teammates, including a white center named Craig Wilson and a light-skinned brother with green eyes, Dalton Sharpe. Dray even once mentioned that one night when he'd gotten loaded with Dalton and Craig, he'd thought about telling them about us, but had quickly come to his senses.

"So what did you ask for?"

"Nothing. The bitch just started giving me shit. Giving me huge tips, tickets, and even some of her jewelry. She told me if I kept this to myself there would be a little reward for me after the baby was born. I don't know who she thinks I'm going to tell. As far as I'm concerned her husband deserves to get a cheating bitch for messing with those white girls in the first place," Jade said with a dismissive wave of her hand. "He doesn't mean shit to me."

"Can I ask you something?" I asked. My

stomach began to rumble with nervous energy.

"Sure."

"What color is your client's hair?"

"Blonde, but I'm sure that it came out of a bottle."

"Does she have any kids now?"

"I don't think so. Why?"

"I was just wondering." My mind was racing a mile a minute. "So you still give her facials and stuff?"

"Yeah, matter of fact I'm going out to her place tomorrow at three for a facial. I wonder what she's going to give me this time," Jade said, tearing a small piece of a dinner roll from the breadbasket.

I couldn't wait any longer. I had to know if she was talking about Dray's wife.

"Jade, what's her name?"

"Judi. Why, do you know her? I hope she's no friend of yours! That girl is wack for sure."

"No, I don't know her." But I did know how her mind worked. I flashed back to Judi in the park, with her air of absolute confidence that she'd taken care of me. I flashed back to all the months of fighting back tears at the thought of losing Dray. That gold digger was the cause of all the heartbreak and depression I'd gone through. And now this valuable information had landed on the table at Willie Mae's Scotch House wrapped more beautifully than a huge box in Tiffany blue. I sank back in my chair, rendered speechless but concocting a plan of my own, and thought about bringing Maurice in to help me. He lived for shit like this.

TWENTY-SEVEN

Before I called Cisco, I checked on the Hornets Web site to see where they were playing. If Dray was in town, I couldn't have my revenge just yet. I was still lying low and didn't want to jeopardize my plan. I was relieved to see that they were playing in Charlotte that night and had a game in Atlanta two days later, which meant they would most likely head to Atlanta after the game rather than coming back to New Orleans.

Cisco showed up at my hotel a little after two, dressed in white warm-ups, a crisp white T-shirt, and a gray-and-black windbreaker. The weather was unseasonably warm, and when I reached for my leather jacket Cisco advised me that my long-sleeved shirt would be more than enough.

"I'm going to take this jacket off as soon as we get to the car," Cisco said. "Now where is it you need me to take you?"

"I need to go out to Kenner. Have you ever

heard of a housing subdivision called Crescent Estates?"

"Yeah, I've heard of it. It's pretty ritzy out there. Matter of fact a lot of ballplayers live there. Is that where we're going?"

"Yep."

"Who we going to see?"

"I just need to take care of some business," I said mysteriously. I knew Dray and Judi lived in a gated community with a security guard but wagered that the guard might think the name Jade belonged to either a woman or a man. If Judi was expecting Jade, then I needed to get there before three o'-clock. I was going to confront this bitch, make her give me back my money, and give me some of hers for charity. I had decided against trying to reach out to Dray to tell him what I knew because of how much it would hurt him. Besides, telling him his wife had been unfaithful to him with one of his friends wasn't going to get us back together.

As we drove down Interstate 10, I tried to picture Judi's face when I showed up on her doorstep. I smiled at the thought of justice being served.

"Looks like our boy might be getting out of jail sooner than everybody expected," Cisco said, playing with the button to his navigation system.

"Who is getting out of jail?"

"Mike Vick."

"How is that?" I asked. I smiled to myself at what Maurice had said about throwing a brick just to get put in prison. I thought how much he would enjoy this misadventure I was going through, and couldn't wait to sit down over some good brandy and tell him all about it.

"I hear he's entering some drug program, which will take some of his time off."

"Smart move and good for him," I said.

"You think the Falcons will take him back?"

"I doubt it. Atlanta is pretty conservative."

"Is it?"

"I think so," I said.

"That's surprising."

"Why do you say that?"

"Everybody calls it 'Black Hollywood.' And a lot of rappers and hip-hop people live there. I think if all the black people got together and said they wanted him back, they might let him come back."

"I don't think it matters what black people want. It's a white man that owns the team and he's going to be listening to what his friends say, and I don't think they want Mike back."

"You right," Cisco said in a low voice.

A sign on the freeway said it was five miles to Kenner, and my nervous stomach began to growl so loudly that you would have never known that I'd had fruit and cereal for breakfast a few hours before. I knew Cisco heard it when he looked over at me with a puzzled expression on his face. I gave him a small smile and was reminded how handsome he was. If I didn't get back with Dray, then maybe I could bring him out. But just as soon as the thought crept into my mind, I heard Maurice's voice chastising me for even thinking about getting into another relationship with a guy not willing to admit that he was sexually attracted to men. I wasn't about to make the mistake of taking Cisco's kindness as a sign that he was interested in dealing with me or his issues about men.

But damn, he was fine, with those big arms and honey-colored skin. He was a little boy and a thug all rolled into one. A nice thug boy.

Cisco interrupted my naughty thoughts. "I think this is our exit."

I noticed a sign for Crescent Estates. "Looks like the navigation system brought us to the right place."

He stared admiringly at the system on the console. "Man, this thing is the bomb. Even though I get sick of that bitch's voice when she trying to take me the long or wrong way. I find myself yelling at her to shut the fuck up because I know where I'm going." Cisco laughed.

We pulled up to a brick security hut, which had a half door on the entrance side. A middle-aged white man in a white shirt and black tie and holding a clipboard greeted us.

"May I help you, gentlemen?" he asked.

I lowered my head in Cisco's direction and said, "We're here to see Drayton and Judi Jones."

"Who shall I say is here?"

"Just tell her Jade," I said. Cisco looked at me like I was crazy. I guess he realized for the first time that I was up to something that might not be strictly legit. But then I didn't expect that would be a big problem for him.

"May I ask the nature of your business? I'm not being nosy — we're required to ask."

"Damn, this place is like trying to get in the White House," Cisco said.

"I'm the interior designer," I said quickly.

"They must be doing some big changes up there, because another designer just came about thirty minutes ago," the guard said with a laugh.

"They're taking bids," I suggested.

"Must be. Do you have their address?"

"2001 Creston Terrace," I said. I remembered the address from the time Dray showed me his new driver's license. He wanted to make me laugh by showing me the picture he'd taken with his tongue stuck out. I always had a good memory for simple shit like that.

"That's right. You just go down to the first stop sign, which is Jacobs Terrace, and make a right and then a quick left. The Jones house is at the end of the cul-de-sac."

"Thanks," I said, waving as we pulled away. As we neared their house, I wondered if I was doing the right thing. In my mad rush I hadn't really thought the situation through. What if she had a maid or somebody else who answered her door? Would I even get inside? It was too late to worry about all that. We pulled into the steep driveway of their two-story mansion. The house was made of cranberry bricks and had two beautiful glass doors. There was a candy-red Mercedes SL sports car with dealer plates from Buckhead Mercedes. I don't know why, but my eyes went to the expiration date on the tags, which read January 28. Somebody had gotten a real nice Christmas gift, I thought.

Cisco switched off the ignition and turned to me. "Now why are we here? Don't tell me it's some friendly visit."

My attention was on the house. "I need to take care of something, but looks like she might have company."

"You want me to go up and knock on the door and find out?"

"Not yet. Maybe we should pull out and wait and see if whoever is driving this car is leaving soon."

"I can do that," Cisco said, starting the engine and putting the car in reverse.

We pulled up in front of the house right next door to Dray's. Cisco and I sat in silence as we watched the house like we were some kind of undercover drug agents waiting for a deal to go down. After about ten minutes, I looked at my watch and saw that it was a quarter to three. The real Jade would be arriving any minute. It was time to make my move.

Just as I was getting ready to tell Cisco to pull back into the driveway, one of the doors to the house opened and a tall and slender light-skinned black man walked out the door. Was this Judi's lover? Jade had said that she thought it was a basketball player, and this person was too short to be playing in the NBA, unless he was a three-point shoot guard. He was wearing sunglasses and a brown warm-up jacket with a hood on his head. He looked carefully in all directions like he was making sure no one had seen him leave the house.

"What do you think dude is up to?" Cisco asked, nodding to the man with his chin.

"I don't know, but he definitely looks like he's up to something."

He jumped quickly into the Mercedes. I thought it was odd that on a day when you could ride around with your top down, this fool was covered up in a hood like a burglar who had just pulled a heist.

Suddenly I had cold feet. I couldn't stoop as low as Judi. Something about the way I was raised prevented me. My plans didn't seem like such a good idea. This was stupid and I needed to just carry my ass back to Atlanta and start over. If this was the person Dray chose to start a family with, maybe I really didn't need him in my life after all. Could be I would give a regular gay guy a chance at my love, find myself a job, and try to live a normal life finally.

We watched as the car slipped out of the driveway. The top started to rise, covering up the driver.

"So what are you going to do?" Cisco asked, almost as much out of impatience as curiosity. "Follow him?"

I looked down the street and saw a pink Volkswagen just like Jade's headed our way.

"Let's get out of here, man. I'm sorry I wasted your time."

"You sure?"

"I'm sure. Let's see if we can follow the Mercedes and find out more."

As Jade pulled into the driveway, Cisco sped off. Moments later we were right behind the Mercedes but at a safe distance, so as not to make ourselves look suspicious. It occurred to me that the driver couldn't be Dalton because he would be with Dray and the rest of the team. But I still wanted to know who had just left Dray's house.

"Why are we following this slow-driving S.O.B. in that nice ride?" Cisco asked out loud to himself.

"We won't follow him for long. Just to the freeway," I said.

"Just tell me what to do, dude."

"Just keep driving like you're doing now. You're doing fine, Cisco."

We followed the Mercedes as it came to the security station. The guard came out and talked to him for a few seconds. The car pulled off, and it was our turn to deal with security.

"That was quick," the guard joked. "I see you didn't stay as long as your competition," he said, indicating the Mercedes.

Cisco gave the security guard a smirk without responding, and then looked over at me. I just looked straight ahead.

When we pulled out of the crossway and headed back to the freeway, the Mercedes was right in front of us. Thank God we were now on a two-lane highway. Cisco sped past. A few blocks later, we came to a traffic light that went from yellow to red so quickly that Cisco had to slam on his brakes.

Looking left and then right, he wise-cracked, "A brotha don't want to get caught out here doing nothing wrong." I looked at him and smiled from a release of tension and nerves; I was happy that I hadn't lowered myself into doing something that would embarrass my mother.

The Mercedes was now idling alongside us, just to my right. I hadn't yet looked over. I was curious to get a better look at the driver but didn't want to be too obvious about it.

Just as the light turned green, I leaned forward casually a few inches and took a look at the driver of the Mercedes. He flipped down the vanity mirror and dramatically brushed his face without looking in our direction, and then sped through the intersection. I was flabbergasted.

"Naw, it couldn't be," I muttered in disbelief.

"What?" Cisco asked.

Before answering I shook my head. Did I just see who I thought?

"Do you know that dude?" Cisco asked, gesturing to the Mercedes flying down the road away from us.

I didn't know how to answer his simple question.

I watched the Mercedes disappear. "I think that's the man I thought was my best friend."

"Word," Cisco mumbled as he sped onto the freeway and back toward my hotel.

TWENTY-EIGHT

A few hours later, I was boarding a Delta flight to Atlanta. As Mama would say, I was spent. Being blackmailed by my boyfriend's wife was hard enough, but seeing my best friend involved both hurt me deeply and left me enraged. I knew Maurice could be an underhanded and low-down bitch when he chose to be, but never would I have imagined he'd turn on me. This realization also left me horribly confused, asking myself not only what I'd done to deserve this betrayal but how Maurice knew Judi. He lived outside Atlanta and it wasn't like he would ever show up for a game. No, this was some major shit that made no sense.

I was more pissed off than I'd ever been in my life, and my thoughts were spinning like a circus ride gone wild. When we'd gotten back to the hotel, I had thrown my clothes into my suitcase and Cisco drove me to the airport in silence. Although he'd repeatedly asked what was going on, I chose to wait to explain the story to him.

We shared a tender moment at the airport. Well, tender for a guy like Cisco. I had stepped a few feet from his car when I heard him call out my name. I turned around to find Cisco leaning his head out the window. With a huge smile, he said, "AJ, everything will be fine. I will make sure of that. I got you, man." He let out a little laugh, waved, and was gone.

My only thought was to get to Atlanta before Maurice did. I was going to pack all my shit and take whatever money he'd left in the closet. Money that belonged to me.

On arrival in Atlanta, I took a cab to Maurice's house and was relieved that it looked like I had beaten him back. Knowing Maurice, he was probably stopping at every small town between New Orleans and Atlanta, trolling the streets in his shiny new sports car looking for boys. He hadn't a clue I knew his deal, and so had no idea what awaited his return. As I pushed the code into the keypad of the garage, I tried to wrap my head around the day's events.

Although I hadn't figured how Maurice and Judi met, suddenly everything made sense. Maurice was the real blackmailer. Some of the information Judi knew about me was in my journals. The journals I'd left in Maurice's care when I moved to New Orleans. That evil sissy had warned me that he could be deceitful and crafty. Why hadn't I been smart enough to see he'd eventually turn his tricks on me?

How could I have been so stupid? Not only with my choice of friends, but about my love life as well? I made up my mind to call Dray and tell him what a fool he was. I was going to tell him that he'd let a good thing get away and nobody would love him like I did. And if he was happy with Judi, well, I was going to tell him they deserved each other.

My battle wasn't with Judi and her nasty ass. It was with the man I had put my trust in, given my love, and more important given my life up for. I decided at that moment, in the empty house I wanted to set ablaze, that revenge wasn't what I wanted. I wanted my own life back and I wanted it now, even if it didn't include Dray.

But first I had to get past something that had happened to me long before I met Dray, something that dated back to my childhood. I located the boxes that held journals I'd started keeping while in high school. Journals that held secrets I thought I'd kept to myself for so long. Journals so valuable to me that I always kept them close by, with the exception of my lapse in judgment when I'd first moved to New Orleans. I immediately found the first one I'd ever had. It was black leather, with yellow pages and blue lines. I turned the pages until I found the entry I was looking for, sat in the middle of the floor, and began reading it for the first time in many years. The memory of that night was now as fresh as a new layer of snow.

It was a winter night, cold and clear, when he showed up. I had just turned fifteen and Bella was two. I was babysitting as my mother worked her part-time job as a sales clerk at the Belk near our house.

His name was Eddie Wilson and I called him Mr. Eddie. He was a tall man, about six-six, light-skinned, with hazel-brown eyes and a five-inch Afro. He took my mother out to the local club a couple of times after meeting her when he came to install a phone line at our home.

I remember Mama telling one of her girl-friends how much she liked Mr. Eddie because he made her laugh, but she was concerned that he was a couple of years younger than her.

On that night I looked out the window and saw Mr. Eddie standing on the porch. I was a little surprised, since he and Mama only had dates on the weekend. I opened the door with hesitation. He asked for Mama and I told him she was working. He asked if he could come in and wait. I let him in.

He flipped through a magazine as I finished up my homework. Every now and then I would glance up at him when I thought he wasn't looking, admiring his handsome face. After about thirty minutes, he looked at me and asked what I was doing. I told him math problems and he walked over to the table where I was studying, saying he wanted to see what math was like these days and wondering out loud if he could do the assignment.

Moments later he was standing behind my chair, peering over me into my math book. I could feel the heat of his body because he was so close to me, and then I felt his breath on the back of my neck.

"Turn around," he instructed me. When I did my face was directly in front of his crotch area and it was bulging. He removed my pencil from my hand. Mr. Eddie then took my hand and placed it on his groin and with his hand on top of mine moved it up and down as he moaned. After a few minutes, he took out his dick and asked me to kiss it. I'd never done that, but

strangely it seemed like the most natural thing in the world.

As Bella slept in the room we shared, Mr. Eddie took me to my mother's room and laid me on the bed on my stomach. He was careful not to disturb the bedspread or pillows as he pulled my pajama bottoms down.

"Have you ever done this before?" he asked.

I turned my head around and looked at him. He had removed his pants and his tantalizing thick dick was hard.

"No," I said.

"I'm going to try not to hurt you," he said as he gently pushed my head into the bed with his strong hands. When he entered me, his delivery was painful but slow and careful. His body shook and he let out a primal scream as he came, pulling his dick out of me, part of his cum in his hand and the rest on my back and legs.

Mr. Eddie went into my mama's bathroom and minutes later returned with a warm washcloth and instructed me to wipe myself off. Then he left, and never returned to see my mother or me.

Reading the entry after all these years made me both sad and angry. Sad because I realized my boyhood innocence had been taken away from me prematurely and mad because the person who'd taken it, like my good friend Maurice, didn't give a damn about me.

My bags were packed and sitting by the front door as I surveyed the room. I wanted to be sure I had everything because I didn't want to have any reason to ever set foot in this house again. All was quiet for a second and in that moment I remembered all the laughter Maurice and I had shared here. The Christmas party suddenly felt like a lifetime ago. Now my mind wanted to bury those moments forever.

The place never felt more silent. I don't know if it was just me feeling especially lonesome after losing Dray and Maurice or whether I just wanted to get out of there badly, but the silence was pronounced.

I walked down the hallway into the living area when I heard the front door open. Maurice's voice shattered my solitude.

"I'm back," he sang out.

A bag of luggage hung from his shoulder and he had on a silly hat with a red-and-green pom-pom dangling from it. He wore a smile that I wanted to slap from his face.

"Did you miss me, hon?"

I stood there in a fury, unable to articulate my rage and deep, deep feelings of betrayal. I held so much resentment at that moment that I thought once I started going off on him, I might end up beating Maurice to the ground.

"Child, did you go deaf-mute while I was gone? I asked you if you missed me."

Coldly I walked passed Maurice and opened the side door that led to the garage. There parked was all the proof I needed: the shiny red sports car with the temporary license plate. I blinked back tears I was determined to suppress and went back inside the house.

Maurice still had on that smile and asked if I liked his new toy.

"How could you do this to me, Maurice?" I snapped. "You of all people. How could you do this to me? What have I ever done to deserve your trying to ruin me?"

"AJ, child, what are you talking about?" Maurice asked in wide-eyed innocence.

"You know damn well what I'm talking about," I shot back. "You and that bitch in New Orleans blackmailed Dray and me. And don't you lie to me. Don't you fucking lie to me! I know it was you. I saw you leave his house today."

He had been busted and it showed on his

face. He couldn't conceal his look of surprise. If I had any doubts about him at all, those doubts were gone.

I reached for one of my bags. I'd never been so disgusted by anyone in my life. "I hope you're happy with yourself, but I hope you know what goes around comes around. So sorry I won't be around to see you get yours."

He snatched the hat from his head and yelled, "Don't you come in here all high and mighty with me, mister. You'll get yours too. It's one thing to be a faggot, but it's another thing to be with a woman's husband and let him take care of you like you're some beautiful white woman. Who in the fuck do you think you are? What makes you think you're so special?"

Maurice moved closer to me, as if he were about to hit me.

"You better move the fuck back," I said.

"Or what? You gonna hit me? Go ahead. I'll call the police so fast you won't have to worry about a place to stay because your ass will be in jail."

"Then get out of my way," I ordered. I didn't know anymore what he was capable of, but I knew Maurice well enough to know that he would follow through on his threat. I had to get out of there before I did something I'd never done in my life: spit in someone's face. He stepped to the side to let me pass and I bent down and grabbed one of my bags.

"Have a nice life, bitch," I said, picking up the second bag. Oh, I would have given anything to slap his ass so hard his head would spin, but I knew violence wasn't the answer. He'd hurt me so badly that I didn't know what could satisfy my fury.

"Oh, I will, thanks to you," he said with bitter sarcasm. "The cash that Ms. Judi gave me for all the information I supplied her with will keep me happy for a long time." He stepped around to my left. "Can you imagine how happy she was to give me some ends when I told her about you? Do you know how much fun I had reading about your little affair and how you couldn't wait until your boyfriend and you were together always? Well, it's not gonna happen, hon. Not now, not ever. Just think of the heartache I saved you."

I was beyond rage by this point. It was obvious I was talking to a madman. "You're sick, Maurice, and I should feel sorry and sad for your pathetic existence."

"Don't feel sorry for me, bitch, because I know who I am. It's you who's got the problem," he said, thrusting an accusing finger at me. "I feel sorry for *your* sick ass. I guess it all started for you when you took your mama's boyfriend. You had the gall to go around thinking you're better than everybody because you got some NBA player to fall in love with you? Just because you don't have to worry about shit, always talking about the charity work you're doing and how you were helping your mama and sister while my ass, like most of the sissies in Atlanta, was out here struggling, trying to keep the bank from taking back my villa."

The depths of Maurice's desperate envy truly shocked me. Sure, he had kidded me about living large, but never would I have guessed that he'd held all this resentment inside.

"You remember that time when I came to see you and you got so mad at me for coming to your house unannounced? Well, I was through with your ass then. I was done. But a bitch like me always got a plan for queens like you. I knew you were most likely sleeping with somebody's husband and I made it my business to find out. I learned about you and Dray almost a week later by camping out a little ways from your condo. I saw who was coming and going. I guess they didn't teach you in North Carolina to never cross a real dirty-south diva because we will cut you, and I mean deep! You sissies think you just hurt somebody and move on to the next victim. But Maurice will never be a victim. Never again, bitches."

Maurice's tirade grew louder and louder in a crescendo of jealousy and resentment. I didn't move, because I was stunned by what I was witnessing but also because I wanted to see how much more of his plan he'd reveal.

"And then you were stupid enough to leave with me all your sleazy little love journals with even more secrets, like how you once had a crush on one of your mother's boyfriends. Do you think she'd be so accepting of you if she knew you wanted to get with her trade? I don't think so." He smiled. "Yes, honey, I found Ms. Judi right before the wedding and we became good girlfriends fast. So she's known about you for a long time. We were both just waiting for the right moment to get back from you what you'd taken from her: her husband! My little film project at the Ritz in D.C. took care of that."

I'd never witnessed such viciousness up close and it was frightening. I felt like I was listening to a stranger who'd been eaten up by malice. This wasn't the world I lived in. We had nothing more to argue about.

"Okay, you win. I'm done," I said as I

started toward the door. I was going to tell him that I had all the money he'd left in the closet but he'd find out soon enough. I was going to take the money and donate a portion of it to Brad Pitt's organization back in New Orleans.

"And don't you dare come anywhere near my party. I will have your ass arrested. Do I make myself clear?"

"Wasn't coming anyway," I said firmly.

"Yes, you are done," he called after me. "Now Judi and her little family can live happily ever after thanks to me. Who knows, she might even ask me to be godfather to the new baby."

It hit me right then that there might be a way to get back at both Judi and Maurice. I stopped in the foyer and turned to face Maurice for one last time.

"So I guess you know the baby's not Drayton's. I'm sure Judi told you, since the two of you are so tight, that she's pregnant by one of his teammates."

"What are you talking about?" Maurice asked.

I simply smiled and walked out the door. My work there was done. If I knew the real Maurice, Ms. Judi would soon feel the sting of blackmail herself.

TWENTY-NINE

I had one more thing to do before I could start my new life. So on the second Thursday in January, I sat in the lobby of the Ritz-Carlton Buckhead waiting for the Hornets team bus to arrive. I needed to talk with Dray and I knew they would most likely arrive, as they usually did, between two and three P.M.

The weather in Atlanta, like the rest of the country, was unseasonably warm but cool enough for me to get away with black straight-cut jeans and a thin white V-neck sweater and black boots.

For me this was a very bold move and something I'd never even contemplated. It had been two months since I'd last seen Dray and I was extremely nervous, yet confident that I was doing the right thing. After years of hiding out and covering up, I was finally closing the door on all that and opening a new one for just me.

Around half past two, the first tall African American man walked into the lobby dressed in an exquisitely tailored suit. He was followed by several men around his height and several shorter white guys carrying bags. The team had arrived and so I put the magazines I was reading back into my briefcase. I stood up and tucked my sweater into my pants, and the few wrinkles on my sweater disappeared.

A few minutes later, Dray walked in. Seeing him so suddenly felt like the time I saw him in college after his first training camp. And I was just as nervously excited now as then. Dray's head was down and he had headphones on. The first thing I noticed was that Dray was wearing the gray pinstripe Armani suit, with a pink shirt and light blue tie, that I had bought him almost a year ago.

I was about to call out his name to see if he could hear me above the iPod, but instead I just stood there. He passed by without noticing me and joined his teammates at the reservation desk.

After ten minutes Dray had finally reached the front desk, and a few minutes later he turned and started walking in my direction. He still looked as if his mind was somewhere else when he suddenly glanced up and saw me. At first he looked upset, his brow wrinkled in confusion or anger, I couldn't tell, but then his face softened almost immediately. Dray looked around, I guess to see if any of his teammates were close by, and then moved toward me.

"AJ! Where the hell have you been? I have been going crazy not being able to get in touch with you," Dray said in a low hushed tone.

"It's good to see you, Dray. How have you been?" I spoke so calmly that I surprised myself.

He moved closer to me, as if he were afraid I might disappear like a ghost. "I thought something bad might have happened to you. You might have been dead for all I knew. I called all the numbers I had for you, even old numbers. I can't tell you how many times I went by the place. You got some serious explaining to do, sir."

"Yes, we need to talk, Dray, but not in the lobby of the hotel," I said.

"Are you staying here?"

"Yes, and I'm listed under my name. Call me when you have time. But if we don't talk before you leave to go back to New Orleans . . . well, I can't be certain we will get another chance."

Dray looked at me like he was trying to figure out who he was talking to, as if a take-no-shit stranger had taken over my body. He just stared at me in wonder and moved his neck back as if he were really seeing me for the first time. "I will call you as soon as I get into my room," he said. "Whatever you do, don't leave without us talking. Please. I can't stand to lose you like that again. I was in a living hell." One of the players called his name, asking if he was coming upstairs. Dray nodded, then headed for the bank of elevators. I waited a few minutes and did the same.

About an hour later, the phone in my hotel rang.

"What room are you in?"

"What?" I asked, not really understanding what Dray was asking me.

"What room are you in? I got about forty-five minutes before I have to get ready to leave for the arena. I want to see you."

"I'm in sixteen forty-eight."

"That's the club floor. You haven't seen any of my teammates in the private lobby, have you?"

"I haven't been there, but my room is at the end of the hall. So we should be cool," I said.

"Okay. See you in a few."

I hung up the phone and took a deep

breath. Why was I so worried? I had clarity about myself and my relationship with Dray more than ever before. I guess I was concerned that Dray might not appreciate this new self-assurance that I would make it on my own.

I went into the bathroom and brushed my teeth, held my hairbrush under cold water, and then pulled it across my head. I looked in the mirror to see if my teeth were clean, if my face was okay. I ran a cold washcloth over my face. I spread some moisturizer over it just as I heard a knock on the door.

I peered out the privacy hole and saw Dray looking down the hallway apprehensively. I pulled the door open.

"Come in," I said.

Dray walked in and wasted no time shooting questions at me.

"Where have you been? What happened to all your phones? Where you been staying? How could you just leave and not tell me? Man, this shit ain't cool. I've been worried shitless. I thought maybe something bad had happened to you. Damn, what are you trying to do to me?"

"Let's sit down and talk," I said, pointing to a pair of chairs. "Let me try to explain." I took Dray's hand and led him to the seats. But instead Dray pulled me close to him and hugged me as if his life depended on it. I inhaled the scent of his cologne as he began kissing me. It brought a load of memories rushing back, which I struggled not to let overtake me. His kisses were deep, like he was making love to me, and I couldn't help but think that maybe I was about to do the wrong thing.

Dray started to go for my zipper and unbutton my shirt when I suddenly stepped back from his embrace and told him to stop.

"What? You don't think we have enough time? I have forty-five minutes," Dray said, checking his watch.

I thought about giving it just one last time, but convinced myself that that was not why I'd come to this hotel. He studied my face and then he smiled.

"Dray, I can't do this anymore," I said.

"What? Meet like this?"

"No, I need to be on my own. What we are doing is wrong and I can't live like this anymore."

"What are you talking about, Aldridge? Have you met someone else?"

"No. It's not about anyone else. This about me and what I need."

"I thought you needed me? Let's not lose what we got."

I didn't answer, but instead stared at Dray

for a moment, my heart still on the fence. It would have been the easiest thing to run into his arms right there.

"Answer me," he demanded softly. "Why can't I be with you?"

"Dray, you know I love you more than anyone in the world, but I think it's best if I just get on with my own life." Speaking those words, I realized that I had hardly ever told him I loved him. I think Dray had said he loved me maybe five times during our entire relationship. Somehow those words felt superfluous when we both knew what we felt in our hearts. Dray looked like he was on the verge of tears, but he didn't cry.

"We're not going out like that," Dray said, his voice quavering with emotion. "You mean too much to me. You're the only guy I ever had feelings for and it can't be over just like that. I won't let it."

"Then you have to make a choice. I can't share you any longer. You have to choose between me and Judi." I hadn't come there to give him an ultimatum and quickly regretted it. What he wanted was no longer my concern. I'd come to tell him what I needed to do.

"You can't ask me to make that decision. I'm getting ready to be a father. I can't just leave Judi now. Give me some time. Let's not do anything until after the baby is born. After that we can talk." He reached out and took my hand. "I'll make things right for you. Haven't I always?"

This was the time I thought I should tell him the truth behind his wife's pregnancy, but I didn't. If I was going to have Dray for myself, it had to be because of how he felt about me, not because he'd married a liar and a tramp.

"There's no time left to talk, Dray. You've made a choice. I wish you well."

"You ain't leaving me. I'm your first and only love. We'll talk about this some more tonight after my game. We'll work something out, AJ, where everybody will be happy. But you can't leave me," he pleaded. "I need you."

"Do you?"

"Yeah, more than anything."

Dray pulled me into him and gave me a small kiss. "I really love you," he whispered. I looked up and saw his private, dreamy smile softening his face.

"I know you do, Dray. Listen, man, it's getting late and you've got to get ready for the game. Why don't we get together afterward?"

"Okay." He smiled as if he'd scored. "We'll order room service and have some great make-up sex."

"Great, babe. Have a good game."

"I know I will, now that I know you're all right." He kissed me again, then headed out of the room. I sat there on the edge of the bed by myself, realizing that I'd be gone by the time the game was over. I felt a good cry coming on, but somehow this time the tears would feel as if they were washing away my old life. I had a whole new future ahead.

I closed my suitcase and prepared to leave my room. I was lucky enough to book a seat on the last flight from Atlanta to Raleigh and couldn't wait to surprise my mother and sister that night.

As I reached the elevator, I suddenly had a question for myself. Is first love the only love? And if so, what did the future really hold for me?

When I got to the lobby, I decided I'd check out by phone the next day so that when Dray called he'd at least get the hotel voice mail.

Walking into a winter night that felt like spring, I couldn't help but notice a half moon hanging securely in the sky. The moon to me was one of God's most romantic creations. I thought about all the times I'd looked at that moon with Dray and how I never would again. It was time to move on. I felt tears coming once more, but with equal speed my mother's words of advice entered my head and I began smiling a smile as bright as the moon itself.

Don't cry because it's over. Smile because it happened.

EPILOGUE

I woke up early one May morning, torn out of a dream about Dray. For the past four months, I'd been staying with my mother and sister, sleeping in my old room. When I woke up suddenly, everything around me felt as still and quiet as a dream itself. It took a second to adjust. In the dream Dray and I were alone on a beach that seemed endless. Nothing but ocean and sand for as far as the eye could see. Walking hand in hand, we didn't say a word. We didn't need to because we were so happy together — happier than I remember us being for a long time. As I lay staring at the ceiling, I wished I could force myself to sleep and return to the dream. But I knew that was impossible.

Love can be like a dream in that way. You're all caught up in it and all about it and you think it will go on forever. You're happier than you've ever been before. Sometimes you don't realize just how happy until it's too late. You wake up, and when that love is over, there's no going back. You can close your eyes, remembering the best of times and maybe even convincing yourself that if you had it to do over again, you know you could make it work, but ultimately none of that matters. You have no choice but to move forward, and moving forward can mean leaving love behind.

That's how I felt without Dray. Leaving him was what I had to do. I knew I'd made the right decision, but that didn't make it any easier. Although four months had passed since we'd last seen each other, I was reminded of him frequently. I couldn't see a basketball in a sporting-goods store or pass a game on TV and not think of him. Occasionally something I saw or heard or read would send me into an especially bad funk that would take hours to get over. It could be something as simple as a song that would play randomly on my iPod or a newspaper ad with a great-looking man. The problem was that I seemed able to recall only our good times together, which made the funk that much worse. I'd begin to second-guess myself, asking if I'd chosen wisely. As difficult as it was to overcome such painful feelings, I learned to pull myself together at these moments.

But it wasn't just obvious things like basketball that brought Dray to mind. Had it been only that, getting over him would have been a little smoother. No, there was also a bunch of stupid stuff that I'd never before associated with Dray but all of a sudden connected with him in his absence. It was a lot like when my grandmother died. Up until her death, peeling an orange was just peeling an orange. Once she was gone, however, I couldn't help but remember how she used to peel one for me at breakfast whenever I spent the night in her home. Today I can't cut open an orange and not think about her. The smell and taste of citrus reminds me of her every time. That's how it was for me with Dray. Ordinary things like the feel of a pima cotton T-shirt or the automobile section of the Sunday newspaper he used to love reading or just some young dude bouncing into a fast-food restaurant all happy could bring intense emotional flashbacks. Who'd have guessed? I hadn't realized till then that the end of a relationship could feel so much like a death.

I found a small amount of solace in the fact that Dray was still worried about my well-being, and realized that I wasn't going to jeopardize his career in the name of love.

One day, soon after I arrived at my mother's, a very handsome man dressed in an Italian navy-blue suit and a sky-blue striped shirt showed up on her doorstep while I was alone. I was startled when I opened the door and saw this clean-shaven man with some of the most glittering, cat-gray eyes I'd ever seen on a human being.

He asked if I was Aldridge, and when I said yes he told me his name was John Basil Henderson, and I immediately recognized the name of Dray's longtime agent. My former lover never mentioned that his agent looked more like a highly successful male model.

John, as he told me to call him, went on to tell me that Dray told him about our little situation, and that Dray had instructed him to write me a check for whatever I asked for. At first I was insulted and angry, but I realized it was Dray's nature to worry about how I would take care of myself.

As John stood in the foyer off of my mother's living room, we eyed each other suspiciously, like players in a chess game, waiting on someone to make the next move. In the stillness and silence I was struck by the strangeness of the moment. I finally broke the silence and told him I didn't want any more of Dray's money.

"He really wants you to be taken care of,"

John said.

"I can take care of myself," I said confidently.

"I'm sure you can. I know it couldn't have been easy for you to give up what you two dudes had," he said with a voice of understanding.

"Is that it, John?"

"Yep. I'm done."

He gave me one of his cards and told me if I changed my mind or ever needed Dray's help, to give him a call. I took the card and before I closed the door on John, and Dray, he looked at me and said, "I'm not new to this kind of relationship, and for what it's worth, Dray told me he cares a great deal for you." I started to tell him I knew that, but I remained silent as I very slowly shut the door.

To help take my mind off Dray as best I could, I threw myself into helping my mother prepare an unforgettable sweet-sixteen birthday party for Bella. It wasn't a *My Super Sweet 16* type of party, but it was close. The quiet time I'd spent with my family had been good for all of us. We'd always been tight, but we hadn't seen so much of one another in years. When I went away to college, we were different people. Bella was a little girl and I was scarcely old enough for my mother and me to share the kind of adult conversations we'd been having all week. I wasn't willing to come out with my entire story — and I'm not sure I was yet emotionally equipped to do so even if I had been — but I offered up enough for her to understand that I'd lost a true love and been betrayed by a trusted friend. She listened patiently as I laid out my troubles. That's one of the things I loved most about my mother: she was so smart that you could tell her only a little, but she could read between the lines and understand the big picture. It couldn't have been easy for her to see her son heartbroken and betrayed, but she didn't let on. Mothers are strong that way.

It was ironic that I would dream about Dray the day I was returning to New Orleans. I'd debated for weeks whether it was the right city to start over in. I wasn't concerned about running into him. I knew it was safe to return when I read online that Dray had been traded to the Detroit Pistons after a locker-room fight. Apparently he'd become combative with teammates following a nasty divorce. The article named his wife's infidelity as the reason for their separation, which meant Judi was going to have one hard time cashing in on her ex. I wondered how Dray looked in his new uniform but was able to restrain myself from going to the Pistons' Web site to look him up. No good would come of that.

Still, there were a number of solid reasons not to choose New Orleans. Apart from the memories of everything that had gone down between Dray and me, there was the fact that I knew virtually no one there. I had grown fond of the town, but wondered if that was enough for me to settle there permanently. My project had been selected by Make It Right to help with home design, but it was only a three-month engagement. When I explained this to Jade — who'd been pestering me to come back — she took the initiative and made a phone call to a friend at Xavier University, who helped me secure a teaching position in their design department. Jade, who was splitting her time between New Orleans and Cleveland, added for good measure that the friend happened to be gay and single and was a dead-ringer for Rockmond Dunbar. Although I'd hoped that teaching at a historically black college might lead to some new friendships, I wasn't ready to date, even if the man in question was a knockout. I was carrying around too many unresolved issues that only time would heal.

However, I was surprised to find myself excited by the idea of meeting a new set of people, and slowly I came to see that it wasn't making friends that was exciting but the realization that for the first time in years I was about to live openly and honestly. No more secrets. But was the exchange worth it? Would I have traded this new openness and honesty for a chance to have the old Dray back? I can't say, and I won't know until I've experienced some of what lies ahead for me.

It seems Judi wasn't the only one to fall on hard times. Maurice saw some bad luck as well. About three weeks ago, I went to Atlanta for the day and bumped into Bobby from the Christmas party outside a Midtown coffee shop. It turned out that Maurice had burned him too, and Bobby was therefore quite pleased to revel in the news that the Glitter and Be Gay Ball had been canceled. He must have noticed the look of surprise on my face because he paused to ask whether I'd heard the news. I shook my head no, adding that I'd been back in North Carolina. He laughed and said — wide-eyed with gossip — that the party being canceled was the least of Maurice's worries. Apparently he'd suffered a spectacular downfall that had set the town buzzing. Dying to know all the details, I asked Bobby to join me for a cup of coffee.

Bobby went on to explain that Maurice had been busted in a sting operation. He'd been getting information on bids for city contractors. His archrival Austin Smith found out about it and alerted the FBI. When questioned by the grand jury about his actions, Maurice — true to his evil core — lied under oath. The perjury charge didn't sit well with his party sponsors, Bobby assured me, and they wasted no time pulling out right and left. They all expressed public concern over how their money was being spent. We shared a good laugh over Maurice's misfortune, and said goodbye. My laugh was an uncomfortable one because despite what Maurice had done to me, I felt there was a person deep inside longing like us all to be really loved.

There was more to the story, I discovered after logging onto Tay's blog for the first time in months. In a posting dated several weeks back, Tay disclosed his troubled past and how Maurice had used it to blackmail him into promoting the party and smearing Austin. Tay also wrote that he was not the first to be blackmailed. Without naming Dray or me, he alluded to Maurice blackmailing a former close friend who was dating a professional athlete. Fortunately the wording was so vague that one would assume he was talking about a heterosexual couple. When he heard about Maurice's arrest, Tay said, he offered to cooperate with the prosecution in any way that might help their case. I pictured a line of cooperative witnesses waiting outside their door. If the prosecuting attorney gets her way, Maurice will be looking for another pen pal — only this time he'll be the one sending letters from behind bars!

I smiled to myself. Well, Maurice, you were always running after notoriety, and you've finally got some. How does it feel, boi? What goes around really does come around.

Boo, child, boo.

ABOUT THE AUTHOR

E. Lynn Harris is a nine-time *New York Times* bestselling author. His work includes the memoir *What Becomes of the Brokenhearted* and the novels, *A Love of My Own, Just as I Am, Any Way the Wind Blows* (all three of which were named Novel of the Year by the Blackboard African American Bestsellers), *I Say a Little Prayer, If This World Were Mine* (which won the James Baldwin Award for Literary Excellence), and the classic *Invisible Life*. His latest book is *Just Too Good to Be True.*

The employees of Thorndike Press hope you have enjoyed this Large Print book. All our Thorndike, Wheeler, and Kennebec Large Print titles are designed for easy reading, and all our books are made to last. Other Thorndike Press Large Print books are available at your library, through selected bookstores, or directly from us.

For information about titles, please call:
    (800) 223-1244

or visit our Web site at:
    http://gale.cengage.com/thorndike

To share your comments, please write:
Publisher
Thorndike Press
295 Kennedy Memorial Drive
Waterville, ME 04901